Out of the Dark Woods

The Tale of Two

Branden Smith

Copyright © 2020 Branden Smith

All rights reserved. Printed in the United States of America. No part of this book may be used or reproduced in any manner whatsoever without written permission except in the case of brief quotations embodied in critical articles and reviews.

ISBN-13: 979-8-6777-2985-0

DEDICATION

To my Grandpa Larry Barber,
thank you for being apart of this amazing journey.

CONTENTS

	Illustrator	i
	Author's Note	iii
Prologue		Pg. 1
Chapter 1	**Detective**	Pg. 9
Chapter 2	**Homecoming**	Pg. 19
Chapter 3	**River Side Road**	Pg. 30
Chapter 4	**The Haunting**	Pg. 42
Chapter 5	**Clarence and Anna Deckler**	Pg. 54
Chapter 6	**The Change**	Pg. 64
Chapter 7	**Mae's Diary**	Pg. 72
Chapter 8	**Man Hunt**	Pg. 86
Chapter 9	**Insanity**	Pg. 99
Chapter 10	**Ritual**	Pg. 104
Chapter 11	**Vision**	Pg. 111
Chapter 12	**Out of the Dark Woods**	Pg. 118

ILLUSTRATOR

Many thanks to Shanna Savage. Your artwork, as always, is amazing. You can find her artwork on Instagram @shanna.letner.tattoo

The Tale of Two

Author's Note

This story is based on factual places but is a work of fiction.

The Tale of Two

PROLOUGE

We were the spearhead of the 55th Infantry Battalion, tasked with advancing an M4 Sherman tank to the war front in Wernberg, Germany. Our platoon's focus was to clear houses and structures near one of the main roads to prevent Nazi encampments and to set up points of support in case the German's decided to advance upon our location. Machine-gun bursts and rifle reports could be heard far off in the distance as my platoon advanced slowly forward through a dried creek bed surround by neatly plowed plots and livestock acreage. A lone, large two-story farmhouse sat off in the distance. A small stone wall surrounded it, blocking our view of the rest of the house.

We began to move at a faster pace as our point crawled out of the creek ditch and took off at a sprint towards the side of the barn, the rest of us followed. Automatically we lined the bottom of the barn for cover as a call came from the front.

"Deckler, Denenberg. Williams, Peter. You're up."

I grabbed the top of my helmet with one hand and held my rifle with the other as I ran forward to the point man. I watched as he peered around the corner of the barn at the farmhouse a few yards from our position. The sound of clinking metal and rubbing fabric came from me and the other men behind as we broke formation and formed up on the point man. The man turned to face us; his eyes showed intense focus as he looked us over.

"You and Denenberg are on point for the back door. Williams and Peter, you have the west side of the house. We will provide cover. Signal when in position."

Without another word, we took off at a sprint around the barn and towards the small stone wall, which we slid into for cover simultaneously. I slowly peeked over the wall towards the lone farmhouse, checking for any kind of movement.

"Alright, move up."

We cleared the wall and branched out into groups of two as Denenberg, and I ran towards the back of the house, and Williams and Peter ran around the west side. Once against the wall and our assigned door, Denenberg ran alongside the wall to peek over towards Williams and Peter. I watched as he signaled something with his hands and turned to look at me, they were in position and ready. I grabbed my rifle with my right hand and turned to look at my platoon leader, who was peering out from behind the barn. I signaled with my left hand that we were in position and ready. He acknowledged back, and the platoon moved forward one by one taking cover behind the stone wall. Denenberg moved his way back towards me as we stacked up on the solid wood door.

"I got the door."

"Copy."

Denenberg gave the doorknob a slight turn to check if it was locked, it was. Gripping his rifle, he turned the buttstock towards the doorknob. Turning to look at the stone wall as a hand appeared from behind it with the signal to breach. Denenberg stood up, and with an ample grunt and a solid swing, he brought the rifle down on the doorknob with tremendous force breaking the door open. I shouldered my rifle as I moved quickly through the door checking the kitchen area which I had stepped into, for any signs of movement.

"Clear," I said loud enough for Denenberg to hear me as I continued to move forward into the next room, which was a wide hallway with a bend to the right. Another "clear" came from somewhere in front of the house as Williams and Peter breached through their entryway. Suddenly a sound of sprinting could be heard down a staircase as someone yelled halt. Denenberg and I moved around the turn to see a man running towards us but turning quickly to open French doors along the left side of the hallway. I pointed my rifle at him as he slammed the two doors behind him. Williams and Peter moved quickly around the opposite corner towards us, with guns drawn.

"We got the bottom floor. Move up to the second." I instructed.

Williams nodded as they turned back, I could hear their boots as they took off up the staircase. Denenberg and I stacked up on the French doors as my heart began to race. I reached for one of the doorknobs and attempted to twist it, but the man had locked the doors shut.

I ground my teeth. "Break it."

Denenberg repeated the same rifle swing on the first door, and the handle broke quickly as I kicked the doors open.

We entered a large parlor room with guns drawn. There was a wooden desk to the right of the room next to a window, bookcases and weird knickknacks randomly spread out oddly with the older books on the cases. A noise came from behind the desk as we drew guns upon it. A gray-haired man appeared clutching a Luger pistol in one hand, and a box wrapped in a burlap sack sealed with twine in the other.

"Put the gun down!" I yelled, aiming my rifle at him.

His pistol hand shook with anxiety as he pointed it back and forth at us. His face the definition of fear. He began to yell at us in a foreign language.

"I will fucking shoot you! Put the gun down!"

"Wait!" Denenberg interrupted. "He is speaking Hebrew! Maybe I can talk him down."

Denenberg spoke as he let his rifle sling take on the full weight of his rifle and held his hands up at the old man. He began to converse with the older man as he stared at Denenberg in bewilderment. The man spoke, still shaking and with gun drawn.

"He says we must leave; we are not safe here."

"Tell him he is not safe here. War will be at his doorstep soon enough."

Denenberg spoke in Hebrew again as the man began to wave his pistol and point it at the door and at the object he held in his hand.

"He says he does not fear war. It's the contents of the box he fears."

"Did he say what's in the box?"

"No, just that we must leave his home."

"Ask him to place it on the desk and lower his weapon, and we will let him go free."

Denenberg spoke again, pointing at the box, the man's emotions became irrational as he forced the pistol forward at us.

"He says we cannot have the box. He is the one to carry its burden."

"What the fuck… I don't have time for this Jewish shit! Tell him to put the box and the weapon down on the fucking desk and get the hell out of here!"

Denenberg raised his voice more demandingly this time and took a step forward towards the old man. Hearing an audible metallic click as Denenberg immediately stepped back and shouldered his rifle. Multiple gunshots fired as I pulled the trigger once. The gun smoke cleared out of the room as the old man lay mortally wounded on the wooden floor.

"Denenberg you alright?"

He held his right sleeve with his left hand as his rifle hung at his side by its sling. I watched as blood seeped between his fingers and ran slowly down his hand. He removed his hand a few inches; it was covered in blood. He flinched and gasped in pain. Boots stomping on wood flooring could be heard as Williams and Peter ran into the parlor.

"What the hell happened!"

"The old man was deranged; he took a shot at Denenberg when I shot him."

Peter walked up to Denenberg to check his wound.

"It's alright, the bullet just grazed his arm. We will take him to the medic and get him fixed up."

He pulled on Denenberg's good arm as they walked out of the room.

"This home is clear Deckler, we should meet back up with the Captain."

"Yeah," I answered back, still staring at the old man who lay lifelessly behind the desk.

As Williams walked out of the room, I slowly made my way forward towards the old man. He lay lifeless with his eyes open, staring at me as if surprised, my bullet had passed through his chest. I glanced him over until I saw the wrapped box. I looked back at the parlor doors as I picked it up and set it on the desk. It was about the same dimensions as a shoebox but a little bit bigger. I began to untie the twine and let it gently slide out of the burlap wrapping that had kept it from sight. It was a beautifully crafted wooden box, probably a keepsake box or a jewelry box with some Hebrew carved on top of it. As I looked it over, it almost felt as if someone was looking back at me.

All this for a box? I thought. I placed both hands on it.

Immediately a silhouette of a deformed creature popped up inside my head as I let go of the box. *What the hell is this?* I stared strangely at the box, but again I placed my hands back on it as if it beckoned me to open it. Slowly I lifted the lid as I felt something indescribable fill the parlor as everything faded into darkness.

CHAPTER 1
Detective

I lit a cigarette as I rode shotgun in that 1945 Ford Police Patrol car, glad we had not taken my personnel vehicle instead with how bumpy this old dirt road was. These damn rocks would have trashed my paint.

"Haven't seen nothing this bad out this way in a long time."

I looked over at the stocky man driving the vehicle. He wore a dark navy-blue police button-up blazer with a slightly loosened tie. He had a full face with slicked greasy hair, and a lit cigarette hung from his bottom lip.

"Come over to Louisville Sheriff, there are plenty of homicides to respond to over there." I chuckled as I took a drag from my cigarette and let out a sigh as the smoke blew out of my mouth.

"They say this one is pretty bad though. Three dead; mother and two children. The husband has been missing for a while now, according to the report."

"Yeah, I heard. Indiana has definitely dumped a handful into my lap with this case."

I took another drag.

"This house is really out in the middle of B.F.E," I stated as I stared out the windshield. Nothing but trees and rocky hillside to my right and a few trees and some plowed land along the Ohio River to my left.

"This ain't nothing." He let out a loud laugh.

"Wait till you get a few counties in from here, there ain't nothing but farmland for miles."

"I prefer my city living, thank you. Never been too much for the country."

As we drove around a bend, you could see a gravel driveway jutting out of the trees to our right. Police cars parked along the road, and the Coroner's vehicle was sitting in the middle of the driveway facing towards us. A police officer greeted us as we began to turn into the driveway.

"Sheriff Jones, good to see you again. And… is that Detective Barnes?"

I leaned my head forward to get a better look at the man standing out of the driver's side window.

"Miller, how you been?"

"Been better. Go ahead and park next to the coroner's car."

We parked the car and got out of it slowly. I corrected my shoulder holster and adjusted my suspenders as I stood up. I tilted my fedora back to get a better view of the smaller raised ranch style home. I rolled up the sleeves of my button-up shirt as Sheriff Jones, and I began to walk towards the house. I studied every detail about it. It was a raised ranch style home, bluish in color with a carport and a room built above that with a large window. The house was built into a side of a hill, and a forest made up the rear acreage of the plot. Its front faced River Side Road and a farm plot that hugged the Ohio River. The front door of the home was just an opening from what I could see. A few police officers were standing around the opening, looking over it and conversing.

A man in a navy-blue suit and white button-up strolled out of the house. He wore a badge on his belt as he headed in our direction. He was an older gentleman with thinning dark hair with grey splotches. He was tall and slender.

"Doctor Oscar, how are yah."

Sheriff Jones stretched his hand out towards him as he grabbed it.

"Sheriff, I am well. Who is your companion?"

"Doctor, this is Detective Barnes."

The man turned to face me. His blue eyes looked seasoned and tired. His nose was slender, and he had a sharp jawline.

"Detective Barnes." We shook hands. "I am Doctor Oscar Harris, the Coroner for this county."

"Nice to meet you, Doctor. I am Detective Barnes Ramirez. How is the situation inside?"

"Three dead and one missing person. Two children; boy and girl on the second floor and an adult female on the first. One child died from blunt force trauma, and the other well… you will see for yourself. The adult female shows signs of possible strangulation. Also, all bodies show wounds similar to a predatory animal attack."

"A predatory animal? What kind of wounds did you see?"

"Incisions produced by claws on all three. The female received bite marks, and a portion of her leg had been mutilated or even possibly eaten."

I looked at the Doctor in his eyes. *A portion of her leg had been eaten?* "What around here could do that?"

"Coyotes, mountain lions, bobcats, dogs. I've seen it all back at the hospital before I started working for the morgue."

"It would have to be a large animal to accomplish a feat of taking on an entire family. Maybe, a dog?"

"Possibly or something larger."

"Sure Doc, it happens from time to time, but animal attacks are not a reoccurring thing in these parts, gentlemen." Interjected the Sheriff as he wiped his forehead with a cloth that he pulled out of his back-uniform pocket.

"It would also be sporadic for an animal of any kind in these woods to get into a house and attack a whole family. Even if it was rabid."

Oscar and Jones continued to converse as my mind began to wonder. I let out a sigh as I messed with my fedora. I turned away from them as I went through different possibilities in my mind. Looking up, I noticed a pickup truck in the carport. *I wonder, is that the only vehicle that the family owns?* The window above the carport also caught my attention. The right side of the window had been smashed, and the hole was half the size of the actual frame. I looked back down at the ground; remnants of glass could be seen scattered in the gravel driveway. I continued to look around for signs of something that had been thrown through the window.

"I see a lot of damage to the exterior of the home. We have a broken two-story window with signs of breakage from inside of the home."

The Sheriff and the Doctor both turned to look up at the window.

I turned slowly, looking around the front yard for an object that might have gone through the window.

"Possibly an object smashed into it, or someone was thrown from it."

"I did not see any signs of the victims showing glass incisions."

"Maybe a point of entry or remains of a struggle on the second floor. What room is that?"

"The master bedroom, I believe. We found the boy in there and the girl in her room on the same floor."

I began to saunter forward towards the carport as the two followed closely behind.

The Doctor cleared his throat. "To be honest with you two. I have not seen a case this bad in my 20 years of working for the Coroner's office."

"The Detective and I were just talking about the same thing earlier in the ride over here. It's a shame about that mother and those poor children. It was only a few months ago that they reported the husband missing."

"I heard about it from the police officers that come to the morgue. Any word on his whereabouts?"

"None. No clues, nothing showed up during the search party. He had just vanished without a trace. We were still looking into the case when we received the call about this."

As we got closer to the carport, I looked over the pickup. It was an older forest green truck, still in good shape, though. It seemed clean for the most part except for some gravel residue along the trim and on the rims. When I looked at the windshield, it had some abrasive marks, almost like scratches. They led down in a vertical motion towards the hood, which had a massive dent in it. I looked back up at the second-story window and down at the hood of the truck to get a proper measurement of what could have possibly been a fall.

"Something came through this window for sure. Something fairly large from these scratch marks and the size of this dent in the hood."

I turned to face the Sheriff and the Coroner.

"But there ain't no objects laying in the yard that are that heavy, and I don't see clues of it being a person. Especially with those marks on the windshield."

The Sheriff walked closer to the truck as he eyeballed the

dent and the scratches. He wiped his forehead again before almost spinning around excitedly.

"Detective! You might want to take a look at this."

I walked over to him as he pinched something out of the windshield wipers between his pointer finger and thumb. He turned and slowly placed it in my held-out palm. It was moist and similar to black leather but not as dried out. When held closer to my face for inspection, a definite order of something foul-filled my nostrils.

"Doctor." I turned slightly to face him carrying the object in my held-out palm.

"Does this remind you of anything?"

He picked it up gently out of my palm with two fingers and studied it.

"Leather or skin, possibly. Though this sample does not have the same characteristics as the human epidermis. Maybe animal, but it would be old by the condition and odor."

"But there ain't no blood Doc. I checked. Just a huge dent in the hood and these marks on the windshield. Maybe they hit an animal on the road?"

As Sheriff and the Doctor continued to debate over the new clue, I continued to walk around the truck. There was a horizontal scratch that ran down the right side of the truck from front to back.

My fingertips traced out the scratch as I walked towards the back of the truck through the carport. Once reaching the back of the truck, I looked up to see the end of the carport. I had made it to the backyard. An old swing set stood in the little yard they had before it was part of the woods. Small trails could be seen weaving in and out of the woods, probably from the children playing and exploring.

 I turned to my right to see a storm shelter entrance that led to the basement. The wooden doors had been ripped up, and one was barely holding on with a single hinge. As I walked closer, I passed another door on the back of the house, but I did not pay much attention to it. I could see a few stairs that led down and a closed-door at the bottom of the concrete block retaining wall. As I looked down at the door, scratches were engraved into the surface of it. *Failed break-in attempt?*

As I went to take a step down towards the basement door. A guttural noise came from the woods behind me, which made me pause. I placed a hand on my holstered pistol as I slowly turned to see empty woods. I scanned the woods long and hard for any movement, but all was quiet. *Probably just a squirrel or bird.* Then a similar noise came again but from the basement door. It was as if something was heavily breathing on the other side as I placed my hand gently on the doorknob and turned it as slowly as possible while leaving my unoccupied hand on my holster. The doorknob would not make a full turn. It was locked.

 "Barnes! You back here?!"

I turned and peered out of the shelter entrance to see the sheriff peering around the carport into the backyard.

"Yeah! Over here, Jones!" I held my hand up as he looked at me and began to stroll over.

"You found something?"

"Appears to be a failed attempt to enter the house through the basement. The door is still locked."

He peered down at me as I stood next to the door examining the scratches on the door. I stroked them to feel the depth and width.

"These are most certainly too big to be a dog."

"Maybe it was one of them mountain lions we were talking about earlier."

"It's a possibility, but I won't know for certain just yet."

"Well, Oscar wanted me to tell you he is waiting in the house. He is finishing up on the female now."

CHAPTER 2

Homecoming

Journal Entry of Mae Deckler No. 1

    Finally getting to use this beautiful leather-bound journal Cyles' Aunt made for me. I do love it so; she is such a sweet lady. She and Clarence have helped our family so much since Cyles was drafted for the war. It's been a rough five years without him, but his family has been there for me and the kids every day it seems. My family comes to visit when they can from Indianapolis, but it's such a far drive for them now that they are getting older. Heck, I am getting older as well! This journal was my 32nd birthday present, after all.

    I am so excited, Cyles wrote that he will be flying in that new airport they built in Louisville in three Wednesdays from now! I am also nervous, but I bought a new dress for the occasion with some of the extra money I have saved up working on Clarence's and Maria's farm. I hope he likes it. It's been five years since we have seen each other, and we both have been through so much—especially him. I wonder how Donald and Bonnie will react when they see him after all this time? Guess we will find out soon.

Our plane touched down at Louisville, Kentucky International Airport that afternoon before the first snowfall. We all hustled off the plane in our Army uniforms carrying large rucksacks full of our living essentials and other things. It had been almost five years since I had been on American soil after registering for the draft. As soon as I stepped off the plane, the cold wind hit me and made my spine shiver. It felt like another foreign country to me as Louisville had an international airport now, which the army corps of engineers built for the war. As I continued onward following the massive group of men in the same uniform as I. My thoughts grew darker as if another person was speaking to me about my new reality.

Alone. Lost. Forgotten.

I put the thoughts aside in my head as I usually did. I needed to adapt to my new environment, I needed to get home to my wife and children. The thought of my wife filled my heart with longing and excitement. It had been many years since I held her in my arms or known intimacy. As airport personnel and soldiers escorted us into the airport building, hundreds of civilians began to cheer for us and welcome us home. Many were girlfriends, wives, kids, and family. My family would not be here. Louisville was too far for them to travel, my wife and two kids alone.

"CYLES DECKLER!"

I snapped out of my thoughts as I stopped in my tracks surround by hundreds of people. I stared around, looking for the familiar voice in the crowd until I saw him pushing his way through. He was a lean man wearing an old baggy button-up shirt and pants with suspenders. He was tan, and his brown hair was graying along with his beard. He stopped right in front of me with the biggest grin on his face as we hugged.

"Dang, look at ole soldier boy coming home looking all spiffy." He let out a yip of glee as he looked me and my uniform over. "Good to see ya back safe, Cyles. The farm has not been the same since you been gone."

"Thank you, uncle, for taking care of the family and the farm till I got back."

"Of course, of course!" He looked me over again, still smiling and let out another noise of excitement as he hugged me back. "My brother would be so proud if he could be here today."

"Yeah," I said, thinking of Dad's face before scarlet fever took his life back in the day.

"Well come now, boy, you know I ain't big on these city crowds, and Mae and the kids are waiting on your arrival back at the farm! She told me, she says, "now Uncle Clarence, please bring him home safe to me once you pick him up from the airport. He has been through a lot, so take it easy on him. Lord knows how bad we all want to see him again."

I smiled and almost shed a tear. "I can't wait to go home."

I placed my rucksack between us on the worn-out bench seat as he got into his old red beat-up pickup truck. The inside smelled of old tobacco as he attempted to start the truck. The vehicle half-ass turned over once and then died once he quit turning the key. My uncle slapped the wheel and mumbled profanity under his breath as he tried to start the truck again. On the second try, it came to life as he whistled through his teeth.

"Hasn't failed me yet! Hee hee. This old girl has been through a lot. Wife wants me to get a new vehicle, but nothing could replace this workhorse I tell yeah."

We began the half-hour drive getting through downtown traffic, mostly in which my uncle's anxiety was through the roof as he gripped the steering wheel tightly with both hands and sat all the way up in his seat. He hated driving downtown as long as I could remember.

"What's it like to be home again?"

"Strange, but I am glad to be back."

"The newspapers and radio told us about the war front over

there. How are you fairing after all that?"

Immediately my thoughts went back to Germany and of my platoon.

"I am doing. I am just ready to get home and get back to a normal life."

My uncle continued to ramble on as we crossed over the Ohio River and into the state of Indiana. A feeling of a pulsation hit my brain like a rock.

Cyles. You will never be normal.

A fear I knew too well now began to engulf me. I could feel it. Like a bug creeping down the back of my neck. Like a cold chill that shoots throughout your spine. Every word gripped my thoughts like an ice pick violently stabbing into ice.

No one will ever accept you for what you have done.

I began to sweat as memories of the war flashed in front of me like a film—every horrid image, every putrid smell worse than the last. I could feel myself sinking into the seat as feelings of convulsions made me turn my neck sharply with a loud crack. I could taste vomit on the back of my tongue as I gripped at my collar to loosen it. It felt as if I was suffocating.

"Boy, you even listening to me, or am I just talking to myself?"

I looked up to see we were driving along an old country road now. The way was gravel and long with farm plots on either side of us. I wiped what felt like drool from my lip on my sleeve as I sat up. I felt groggy.

"Sorry uncle must have dozed off."

"Did I put you to sleep with all my talkin?" He chuckled.

"My wife says I ramble on too much sometimes. I could even put the pigs asleep with my talking, she says. They sleep all the time anyway, so it's not like it would matter."

"No, it's not you. Just tired, it has been a long time since I have gotten some decent sleep."

"I could tell. When I first picked you up from the airport, I noticed you had some dark circles under your eyes. Must have been hard with all that traveling and whatnot."

"You could only imagine."

"Well, you about to go home and sleep good tonight." He chuckled and made a wink at me.

"Yep. Gonna make the little wife pleased as punch, I bet."

I shook my head. It's been some time since I slept with anyone else in the same bed as me. I am not sure how I was going to take to it since it has been so long. I longed for my wife though, we would talk about it in letters a lot while I was overseas. She reassured me all the time that she felt the same way.

"Your bag fell off the seat earlier. We hit a bump in the road, and it flew right off. I picked it up for yea. This box almost fell out…"

My heart jumped to my throat as I could feel myself becoming irritable.

"Nice looking thing. Had some symbols on the top. Is it-" I cut my uncle off.

"Did you touch it?"

"The bag? Yeah, I picked it up."

"NO, the box."

"Hey, now, Cyles, I didn't go through your bag. When I picked up the bag, the flap was open, and I saw the box sitting on top…"

"THE box, Uncle. Did you touch it?"

"Well, no. I didn't. I just saw it and was…"

I immediately grabbed my bag and set it in my lap as he continued to ramble on. I flipped the top flap back and revealed the oak box that was still closed and latched with its burned Hebrew engraving at the top. The wax letter seal I placed on the side of the box was still intact as I let out a sigh of relief and swallowed my fear down my throat. Then immediately, I became enraged as what I felt like an invisible knife stabbing me in the back of my neck with a burning feeling that changed my emotions.

Hate. Kill.

"The box is mine, you hear me. What's in this box is none of your concern, and I would appreciate it if you would never bring it up in conversation again."

"Okay, Cyles." He said as he glanced at my face while driving with a concerned look.

"I did not mean to offend; it was only a question."

"Well, don't."

I placed the box back into my rucksack and put it between my legs on the floorboard. I closed and buttoned the top of my backpack roughly and sat back in my seat. We both sat quietly for a while as I watched farmland and trees go by out the window as we continued down that long gravel road. My uncle broke the silence.

"I know you must have gone through a lot over there, boy. But your home now, the wife and I are always here for you and your family."

I let out a sigh as I turned towards him as he glanced between me and the road.

"I am sorry for my outburst; I am just tired, and everything is different."

"I know, but your family is here for you. You don't have to go through anything by yourself anymore."

"Thanks."

I attempted a smile that was not genuine. As I felt the truck make a left turn, I looked up to see a familiar old white two-story farmhouse along the Ohio Riverbank. Farm plots set on both sides of the home, and its front door faced the woods across the road. A red tractor sat next to a familiar green truck as chickens weaved in and out between the two.

"Welcome home, Cyles!"

As we pulled up in the gravel driveway, I sat up in my seat as a woman with brunette hair stood on the front porch holding the screen door open peering out at our truck. Before the truck even had a chance to stop, I had grabbed my bag, opened the door, and leaped out at a sprint for the beautiful woman. She started to jog towards me as the screen door slammed behind her. I watched as her hair flowed with the wind that engulfed her as she ran. We embraced as she cried in my arms, and we kissed several times. I looked up behind her to see two children standing at the porch looking at us as she cried into my uniform. I studied them both in awe as I slowly began to realize who they were from a distance.

"Mae is that… Donald and Bonnie?"

She looked up at my face with her brunette hair sticking to her pale skin, and her blue eyes sparkled with tears.

"Yes, Cyles... that's our kids."

I slowly let go of her as I stumbled my way over to them, never taking my sight off them. She followed closely behind as I stopped right before the porch stairs. I looked them both over. Bonnie, my daughter, who must have been seven years old now, stood there with her dirty blond hair blowing with the cold wind. She had her mom's blue eyes and features. Donald, my boy, had light brown hair and brown eyes like me. I studied them both until Mae broke the silence.

"Kids, this is Cyles, your daddy, who left for the war after you were both born."

She placed her arm through my right arm and held on to me tightly as she motioned at them both to step down off the porch and come to her side. They both slowly stepped off the porch, and cautiously walked towards me like I was the worst kind of stranger.

I neither felt pain in my heart or sadness as they approached me like I was a predator. They were as much of a stranger to me as I was to them. The last time I saw them, which is barely even a memory now, one was a toddler and one an infant. Little did I know that homecoming would not be what I imagined it to be. Everything was completely different now; I am different now.

CHAPTER 3

River Side Road

Sheriff Jones led me through the front door as the police officers standing out front glaring and conversing over the smashed-in front door stepped out of the way to make room for us. Through the front entrance was an immediate staircase that leads to the second floor. To the right was a living room area with a couch facing a fireplace, a window to the right, and a radio standing underneath the window. The left side of the staircase opened into a kitchen where another police officer stood watching as the noise of a camera flash sounded. The whole first floor smelled of metal and a blood trail ran from the living room into the kitchen entrance and to the right, behind the cabinetry.

I slowly made my way into the living room, studying the

blood pattern on the floor. It wrapped around to the left of the staircase. A decorative table stood parallel to the wall. Smashed glass covered the floor, and a small pool of blood could be seen splattered beneath it. I bent down and picked up a piece. It was a triangular piece that was on the larger side. It was thick in width and had sharp edges from the break. I looked around to get a better understanding that it was a piece of a large smashed vase. *The victim in the kitchen must have used this large vase to fend off her attacker.* I placed the piece back on the ground, where I picked it up as I continued to search around the room.

In front of the living room couch appeared to be a long black skinny pole. As I walked around the sofa, I saw the object in its entirety. It was a fireplace poker. I looked up at the fireplace to see that its tool rack had been knocked over. All the other tools were still near the stand except for the poker. I picked it up off the ground to feel the weight of the iron it was made of, a piece of what appeared to be black leather stuck to the left prong that made up the poker's head. As I brought the poker prongs closer to my face, I realized the black leather like material was the same as the one we found on the truck outside. *She must have stabbed the assailant with this poker, which could explain the blood. But it appears as if something was dragged from this living room and into the kitchen by the way the blood pattern smears and trails off.*

I placed the fireplace poker back down and stood up. I began to follow the blood trail out of the room and into the kitchen. A police officer stood in the entranceway that leads into the kitchen, his eyes still studying something on the floor as he held his hat against his chest. He turned to look at me as he noticed me walking his way. His face was pale white, and his brown eyes were almost the same color as his mustache. I showed him my badge.

"Detective Barnes Ramirez, Homicide."

"Detective. I am Officer Brice Puller."

We shook hands as he let me squeeze into the kitchen next to him to get a better view of the scene. A younger women's body lay on the floor, facing towards the ceiling. Her brown hair laid sprawled and soaked in the blood that was on the kitchen floor. Her blue eyes lifeless, and her skin had begun to change color to show postmortem changes in her body. Her clothes were stained in blood, and she had large gashes on her torso and one on her face that was deep enough to show tissue and her skull. Her right leg was mutilated to the point that I would have just called it her tibia and fibula. Her throat was a shade of purple. A camera flash almost startled me as I was deep in thought.

I looked up to see Doctor Oscar holding a camera and taking pictures of different parts of the victim's body.

"Who's the women?"

"Mae Deckler. Age 34. Cause of death, hemorrhaging."

"What about the bruising on her throat?"

The Tale of Two

"Done before death, appears someone was attempting to strangle her. That's not the important bit, though. Look at the right leg."

As I looked down at the leg, it was just a bloody bone with strands of flesh and muscle hanging from it.

"You're going to need these," Oscar said as he handed me a pair of medical grade gloves.

I stretched them onto my hands with a snap as I continued to study what was left of the right leg.

"Grab hold of what is left of that muscle right there." He pointed with a gloved index finger.

I grabbed a shred of muscle and pulled it taunt with a cringe at the sound my actions produced.

"See those tares there. Along with what's left of the skin and the muscle."

They were more like shreds of cheese then tears. It was like someone took a metal rake to Mae's poor leg and skinned it right down to the bone.

"Those are not cuts made by any tools. Now flip it over and look at the epidermis."

Doing as instructed, I flipped it over to her white flesh. The doctor rubbed some of the blood off with his thumb to reveal small indentions with bruising.

"Those Detective are bite marks. The way I know these are not human bite marks is that they don't resemble a small oval shape. The circumference is much larger, and the depth of the bite is deeper than the average humans."

"I see. These marks here that are part of the tearing, they are also indentions of the bite?"

"Precisely. Which is why I believe that the leg was eaten by an animal."

Brice shook his head at the statement with a covered belch and turned away from the sight.

"A damn shame. Mae was a fine woman, and her husband was a good man as well."

I turned to look at Brice, still leaning over Mae's body letting go of the shred of tissue and skin.

"You knew the victim?"

He turned back around to face me. His face was a light shade of green now.

"I went to grade school with her. She had gone on to marry Cyles Deckler, her highschool sweetheart. She and had two kids with him before he left for the war. I even came by the house a couple times to purchase fresh produce with the wife and son."

"Did you know Cyles like you knew Mae?"

"Not as well as Mae, but enough to consider him a friend. Why? Do you think he had something to do with this?"

"That goes unseen for now, but he is a suspect. We have a wife and two children dead and a missing husband. Has Cyles ever been arrested?"

"Once Cyles was arrested for driving under the influence while coming home from a bar in New Albany in that same green pick-up truck outside."

"Any other reports?"

"Not that I can think of off the top of my head. For the most part, he was an average farmer. Always willing to help anyone in need. Even helped me pull my truck out of a snow ditch once. He was usually always a happy individual. That was before the war, of course."

The camera flashes in the background as the doctor continues to work.

"Do you mean he changed after his return from the war?"

"I am not sure if that's the word I would use, but yeah. Cyles seemed different somehow. Distant. The war is over, but to me, he seemed as if he was still fighting every day."

"I've seen that a lot in combat veterans that have returned.

They have difficultly readjusting to being home. Did you know who questioned the witness that reported the crime?"

"I believe that was Officer Miller. He was one of the first to arrive on the scene. The witness is the Uncle of Cyles Deckler. Clarence Deckler. He and his wife own a farm a few houses down the road from here. But If you don't mind, detective, I need to step outside and get some fresh air."

"Thank you, Puller. I will come to find you if I have any more questions."

He nodded his head as he stepped out of the kitchen and went out the front door.

"The new ones always have trouble with this sort of thing. Takes a few years of experience to get used to murder scenes."

"Isn't that the truth Doctor, but the job never gets any easier. Especially if you know the victims."

Oscar shook his head while picking up a sizeable bloody knife that laid next to Mae's body.

"I found this next to Mae when I arrived, I still need to take fingerprints to be sure, but I believe she used this to deter our vicious assailant."

Focusing on the blade in his hand, I stood up and began to look around on the countertops. Next to the stove was a knife block set. Bloody handprints were smeared on the counter and on a few of the knives in the set. *Mae must have struggled to obtain a knife from the block.* I continued to look around the kitchen to see a few more bloody handprints on the counters closest to the front door. Turning around to face the back of the kitchen, which had another entryway that leads to what looked like a small hallway, the kitchen did not have any more handprints, but small blood platter streams could be seen on the walls. I studied the blood splatter until my eyes focused on a strange smear on the molding of the entryway. Maneuvering around the Doctor as he continued to map out the crime scene, I walked closer to get a better look. The blood smear on the molding was much longer than the average human handprint, and there was gouging where the fingers would have been. *Could an animal really leave behind a blood print like this?*

"Detective."

I turned to see Sheriff Jones stepping into the kitchen.

"One of my officers found evidence of an attempted break-in around bac…" He paused as he saw the remains of Mae Deckler.

His face made a little contortion as he let out a sigh and closed his eyes.

"Lord, who would do such a thing?" He wiped his face in a downward motion with his hand stretching his face.

"You were saying, Jones?"

"Around the back of the house. The back door has the same marks as that cellar door we were looking at earlier."

"I will head back there now to take a look."

"I will come with ya. I am not too fond of seeing women in such a state. Makes my blood curdle."

We walked out of the kitchen and turned a sharp right into the small hallway. A wooden bookshelf stood in front of the back door that appeared to be open, just a crack. As we got closer, there were scratch marks on the bookshelf closest to the opening and the molding of the door itself. Jones watched as I inspected the bookshelf and the cuts in the frame.

"Appears something was trying to claw its way in."

Looking down at the ground. I could see that the bookshelf was pushed from the right side of the door because of scratches on the wood floor. I began to push the bookshelf to the right of the entrance to test its weight. To my surprise, it was quite heavy and made of solid wood.

"Sheriff, you mind giving me a hand with this bookshelf."

He nodded as we positioned ourselves on the left side of the shelf and began pushing it away from the door. It moved with some force to the side as it scratched against the wood floor. The sheriff gave a grunt as we cleared the back doors obstruction.

"Ain't no way that little lady in there could have pushed this bookcase by herself."

"She must have had help from the two children, or at least one of them."

I placed my hand on the doorknob as I slowly pulled the door open. The cool afternoon breeze rushed from the woods and through the doorway, with it a stench of something unfamiliar. As I stepped out on the two concrete steps which led out of the door and into the backyard, the Sheriff followed closely behind.

"Smells like there is something dead in the woods."

I stopped on the second step to get another good look at the backyard. Everything appeared the same as earlier. The old swing set still stood in the same place, but the smell still lingered as I looked to the right to see the storm shelter entrance that I inspected earlier. I turned around to face the Sheriff, who was still standing in the doorway as I remembered something that Officer Puller said earlier.

"Is Officer Miller still working in the front yard?"

"Yeah, they got him working the perimeter. Why?"

"Puller told me he was one of the first on scene and had spoken with our witness that reported the homicide. I need to speak with him and the witness."

"Well, let's head back around front."

As he turned to walk back through the house, I followed. Making our way through the living room, the Sheriff was doing his best to avoid the scene in the kitchen as we walked out through the front door and past the Coroner's vehicle. Puller was standing near the end of the driveway, smoking a cigarette as he looked out towards the Ohio River.

"Miller."

He turned around to see the Sheriff and myself making our way slowly through the front yard towards him.

"I knew you would be out to talk to me sooner or later, Barnes." He said as he threw the cigarette in the driveway and snuffed it out by placing his shoe on top of it and scooting his shoe backward.

"How is it going out here? Anyone try to stop and see what's going on?"

"A few cars slowed down, but no one has stopped to ask yet."

Approaching Miller, I shook his hand.

"Officer Puller told me you were one of the first on scene and got to speak with the witness personally."

"That's right. I spoke with Clarence Deckler after arriving on the scene. He was distraught about the whole thing you can imagine.

Seeing his nephew's family butchered and still not knowing where his nephew is."

"Did you get his phone number and address."

"I did. I got it right here on paper." He pulls a folded paper out of his uniform breast pocket and hands it to me.

The paper reads.

8132 River Side Road

Elizabeth, IN

The phone number was written underneath the address.

"So, he lives only a few houses down from this one?"

"Yep. Clarence said he and the wife would be standing by the phone for when the detective arrived on the scene for questioning. There is a phone in the house near the back of the kitchen."

"Detective you go give him a call. I am going to smoke real quick."

Giving the Sheriff a nod, I slowly made my way back to the house as I looked at the address and phone number once again. *This case is becoming stranger by the minute, what kind of animal could have done this? Maybe it wasn't just an animal, and it was a person as well. Perhaps the witness can help shed some light on this case, and whatever was in store for me on the second floor.*

CHAPTER 4

The Haunting

Journal Entry of Mae Deckler No. 2

Cyles has finally returned home! He was so happy to see me; he almost got ran over by Clarence's truck trying to get to me! I think he and the kids will need some time to adjust to each other... it's been quite odd. But they will come around once they have had some quality time and an adjustment period, I am sure. I am a little sad about the dress though, it got ripped the first night, and I do not think he even noticed it. Cyles has become a bit rougher around the edges, than I remember... he used to be so gentle and heartfelt. I think something has changed about him, but I can't place my finger on it. Or maybe I have changed, or it's just been so long. I hope once he adjusts to having the kids and me around once again, he will return to my old Cyles. Anyways, I am just glad to have our family back together!

Startled out of my sleep, drenched in sweat, my heart racing as I exhale and inhale sharply. I look around the dark room frantically to see Mae sleeping soundly next to me in our bed. Not even disturbed by my night terrors. A calm relief comes over me as I watched her sleep soundly as I caress her hair out of her face. I get up out of our bed, doing my best not to disturb her sleep and gently place my bare feet upon the floor, so it does not squeak. I quietly open our bedroom door to the welcoming darkness of the second story hallway. Making my way to the bathroom, which is right outside of our bedroom to the left. I look to my right to see Donald sleeping soundly in his room with his door wide open. I grab the doorknob and slowly close it shut, doing my best to not make a sound. I walk into the bathroom and turn on the light as I look at my face in the mirror. My medium length brown hair a mess, and my eyes bloodshot with dark circles under them. I am wearing a white tank top with just my boxers on.

Closing my eyes, I take a long sigh before turning on the water to wash my face. I reach for a towel opening my eyes to see a hideous creature staring back at me through the bathroom mirror. Its face is grey and decaying, and its teeth are sharp and pointed as blood pours out of its mouth. I almost let out a yell before clasping my hand over my mouth and closing my eyes. When I open them once again, it is just my own reflection in the mirror. Gripping the sink with both hands, I do my best to let my breathing relax. A sound echoes up the stairs from the first floor. A hallow noise like someone left a window open and the wind is blowing into the house.

I pass Bonnie's closed bedroom door to the left of me as I turn and slowly make my way down through the dark staircase seeing only the moonlight from the front door lighting up the wood floor at the end of the last stair. Suddenly one of the doors on the first-floor creaks open loudly as I pause to listen. My heart begins to flutter. Silently as possible, I rush down the stairs and turn right into the kitchen to find a flashlight in one of the drawers. I hear the creaking noise again as I turn on the torch, and it illuminates the kitchen. *It must be the cellar door.* I make another right out of the kitchen past the backdoor and to the basement, underneath the staircase. The door is wide open as I shine my light upon it. My mind begins to race as I start to feel lightheaded.

Come.

Without hesitation, I began the descent into the basement as the door slowly closes behind me. The cellar is dark and cold as I make my way down the wooden stairs. My flashlight begins to blink the closer I get to the bottom, smacking it a few times it finally goes out as darkness surrounds me.

"Shit."

Looking up, I see that the bottom of the stairs that touches the concrete floor is illuminated by a soft blue light. Stepping on to the basement floor, I turn into the cellar to see an outline of a human floating above the floor. The specter glows a soft blue and is transparent. Its features cannot be distinguished besides its basic shape as it stares at my rough sack that is lying against the wall. To my surprise, I am not afraid as I gaze upon the ghost who has now raised his hand, slowly pointing at the bag. My mind begins to become fuzzy again as I turn to look at the bag.

Retrieve the box.

I watch myself, in what appears to be the third person now, make my way over to the bag and open the top flap and pull out the wooden box.

"No. Stop. Your family is in the house." I say to myself, who is now holding the box with both hands and looking up at the ghost. The specter slowly turns away from me as I follow the spirit to the preserve pantry I am building for my wife. The door I installed into the false wall opens by itself, letting the specter in, and my third-person self follows. I try to jerk forward to stop myself, but I am frozen in place as I watch them both disappear through the door and behind the false wall.

The outside cellar doors burst open as the pantry door shuts closed softly. The room becomes cold as I can see my breath with every exhale. *What the hell is happening?* An unearthly low growl that makes my skin crawl can be heard as the second door leading outside begins to creak open. I watch paralyzed in fear as a figure blacker than the night itself steps into the entryway producing horns of a ram and a stubby lower body. Its hoofs clicked against the concrete as it slowly makes its way into the cellar and turns to look at me. As it huffs violently, its breath can be seen in the dark along with its yellow eyes and vertical black pupils. I try to scream, but it feels as if I am being choked. The creature starts to make its way slowly towards me as I do everything in my power to move. A familiar voice sounds all around me.

"Cyles. Cyles honey, wake up. You're having a nightmare, wake up."

I begin to talk again as the creature starts walking at a faster pace towards me, huffing more violently.

"Mae. Help me. I can't move."

"Cyles your dreaming, wake up. I am right here. You have to wake up."

The creature lets out a horrible scream and lunges towards me as I begin to yell.

I jerk awake. The sunlight fills my eyes as my blurred vision focuses on the person in front of me.

"Cyles, are you okay? You were having a terrible night terror."

As my view becomes clear, I see Mae standing above me,

looking worried. Her brown hair shimmering in the sunlight and brow crinkles with stress.

"Did I wake you with my nightmares again?"

"No. It's almost lunchtime. I was letting you sleep because I know you have not been sleeping well the past few nights that you have been home. Was it about the war again?"

"No, just a nightmare this time."

"I am sorry. But, I appreciate you staying up late last night to finish my preserve pantry in the cellar, but I rather have you get more sleep."

Late last night? I went to bed right after Mae did.

"I am sorry, Mae. I just haven't been able to sleep lately, so I figured I would work on your pantry to tire myself out."

"I care more about you getting enough sleep every night then my pantry. You have all the time in the world now to complete it, now that you are home for good."

Her words played in my head like a repeating record. She leaned down and kissed me while I was still lying in bed.

"I am making lunch. Get dressed and come down to eat with the kids and me."

I watched her as she turned and walked out of our bedroom

and down the hallway. Letting out a huge yawn, I was still confused about what she meant working late last night on the pantry. I stopped working on it around ten and went to bed right after she had fallen asleep. Shrugging it off, I proceeded to get out of bed and get dressed.

Trying to talk to the kids at lunch was still an awkward process for me, but they seem to be warming up to me, the more I try. It has only been two weeks since I've been home, and everything is still strange to me. As the kids ran out the back door after Mae told them they could play outside in the back, I got up and took my plate to the sink. As I cleaned it, I heard the door that led to the basement open ever so slightly. Leaving the faucet running, I walked out of the kitchen and into the connecting hallway that led to the basement door and the living room. The door was slightly open as I turned to look out the back door. The kids were running around in the trails they had made in the woods closest to the backyard.

I turned back to see that the door was open a little wider now. I rubbed my eyes as I walked towards the door. *My eyes must be playing tricks on me again. Mae is right; I need to get more sleep; I must just be imagining things from lack of sleep.* Grasping the door handle, I opened it the rest of the way as I made my way down into the basement, turning on the hanging light bulb above the stairs. I get to the bottom of the stairwell and place my feet upon the concrete floor, I get this feeling as if I am not alone. It felt as if someone was watching me as I walked across the basement towards the new pantry I am installing.

Goosebumps formed on my arms and legs as the temperature of the room changed. Pausing as I began to see my breath with the cold, I stared at the pantry with concern.

Something had changed about it, almost overnight, but I could not place it in my mind. *My dream could not have been real, I was in my bed when I woke up this morning.* I turned, remembering my rucksack being opened in my dream, which still laid against the wall where I left it. A shiver ran down my spine as I saw that the top flap was open. Immediately I ran towards the pack and rummaged through it. The box was gone. My mind began to race as I thought about all the possibilities that could have happened. *The kids found it, and we're playing with it outside. My wife had taken it, going through my bag doing laundry.*

My ears began to ring as a headache formed between my temples. I placed my hand against my nose as I felt it start to run. Looking at my hand again, there was blood. *Where the hell is the box!* The dream I had last night slowly came back to me in detail. *Maybe it wasn't a dream, after all.* I turned around, still holding my hand to my nostrils as I walked towards the pantry. I placed my hand gently as I turned the doorknob, and the door opened with ease as I walked into the dark pantry and closed the door behind me.

*****

"Come on, Bonnie, it's getting late! Mom will get mad if we are not washed up before supper!"

I brushed my long brown hair out of my face as I watched my sister come skipping down the trail towards me.

"I'm coming!"

"Let's go through the basement, so mom doesn't see that our shoes are wet from playing in the creek."

"Okie Dokie." She replied with a snicker as she reached for my hand.

"Is dad still working on the pantry for mom? Won't we get in trouble if he sees us?"

"Nah, we would have heard him working on it if he was down there." I pronounced as I held her hand.

We both opened the two cellar doors as we walked down the concrete stairs to the door that led into the basement. Bonnie stood in front of the basement door as I closed the cellar storm doors.

"Hurry, I don't like the dark!" She whined.

"I'm hurrying, I'm hurrying."

I walked past her through the dark and began to open the basement door quietly as possible, just in case someone was in the basement. I peeked inside to see that only the staircase light was on.

"Okay, lets hurry and put our dirty clothes in the laundry, change, and make our way upstairs."

She whimpered yes as we walked into the basement and slowly closed the door behind us. As we walked towards the laundry sink, I noticed how abnormally cold it was in the basement. Bonnie's teeth began to chatter as we did our best to hurry and wash up in the sink.

"What is that red stuff on the floor?" Bonnie asked as she shivered from the cold.

I turned away from the sink to see what she was pointing at. It looked almost like blood drops; I knew that it was once I got closer to it because I cut my hand once playing with one of mom's knives from the kitchen. The blood trailed off towards the new pantry door.

"Bonnie, hurry up and get upstairs," I told her as I began to walk towards the closed pantry door.

"Why? What's wrong?"

"Nothing, just go upstairs."

As I began to slowly reach for the doorknob. Something behind me crashed that made me jump, and my sister let out a high-pitched scream. I turned around to see a box of nails had fallen to the floor near the staircase, my sister stood right next to it.

"Bonnie, did you do that!?"

"No! It fell by itself! I can't even reach the top of the cab…" She froze in mid-sentence as her face turned ghost white, and her mouth dropped open as she stared at something behind me.

I turned around to see dad standing in the now open pantry door. His face was red as he looked us both over. I felt my heart jump into my throat.

"So, it was you two."

"Me… we…" I stuttered to get my words right.

"You two were playing in the basement again after I had told you not too and then…"

He paused, his face almost seemed to morph as the anger inside him rose.

"You took my box."

"Box? What box… we just came in from out…" He snatched me up by my collar with one hand as I tippy-toed off the concrete floor.

"You know damn well what box! You took it from my rucksack over there against the wall."

Fear spread throughout my body as I began to shake. Staring into his eyes gave me a feeling like I was being looked through or that he was not actually my father. I began to shed a tear as I mumbled, trying to tell him we didn't touch his box. My sister began to cry and ran upstairs. He let go of my collar as I fell back onto the floor.

"I don't ever want to see either of you two down here again!"

His voice morphed as he yelled. "Now, get out!"

Without hesitation, I immediately jumped up and ran upstairs while tears streamed down my face as I heard the pantry door slam closed. Once I got up to the top of the stairs, and into the small hallway, I slammed the basement door shut behind me and laid my back against the door. I began to cry as my back slid down the door, and I landed on my butt. I reached for my stretched-out shirt collar when I noticed a burning pain shot down my back. I bent my hand backward and reached my hand up the back of my shirt as I felt three lines running down my back. I began to cry as I touched them. They were scratch marks like something had clawed me from behind. *What just happened? Was that even my dad?*

CHAPTER 5

Clarence and Anna Deckler

I held the phone in my left hand and punched in the phone number with my right. The smell of blood still filled the kitchen as the Doctor was zipping up Mae's body in a body bag and preparing to move it with the help of a few police officers to his vehicle before continuing to the second floor to work on the two children. The phone began to ring as I pinned it between my left ear and shoulder as I transferred the parchment to my right hand. Rereading the address. 8132 River Side Road Elizabeth, IN. The phone made an audible click as someone on the other line picked up.

An older man's voice could be heard. "Hello?"

"Hello, this is Detective Barnes Ramirez with Louisville

Homicide. Am I speaking with Mr. Clarence Deckler?"

His voice cracked as he sounded like he was holding back tears. "Yes, Sir, it is."

"I was told by Officer Miller you were the one that called in the report?"

A second feminine voice could be heard in the background. "Is it the detective? Clarence?"

"Yes, it is, but hold on a second, I am talkin. Yes, Sir, I was stopping by to check on my nephew's family today, like I usually do since his disappearance. I pulled up in their driveway when I noticed the window, and the door was smashed. I ran into the house as fast as I could and found..."

He began to choke on his words.

"When you found Mae Deckler?"

"Yes, Sir. I found her first and then ran upstairs to see... I am sorry, I can't bring myself to talk about the children." He began to sniffle over the phone.

"I understand you are going through a difficult time Mr. Deckler. To make this easier on you, I will just ask you a few questions, and you do your best to answer them so we can help you to the best of our abilities."

"Okay."

"What time did you arrive at the house?"

"Right after breakfast, around seven or eight, I think."

"Had you noticed any significant changes in the Deckler family before or after Cyles' disappearance?"

"No, besides from Mae, and the kids have been worried sick over Cyles."

The second voice spoke again in the background. "I did, I had been talking to Mae several times a day after the disappearance."

"Well, get on the phone, woman, and tell him what she said."

I heard the phone being passed as she spoke up.

"Hello Detective, I'm Anna Deckler. The wife of Clarence and the aunt of the family."

"Good afternoon Ma'am. I am Detective Barnes Ramirez, Louisville Homicide. You were saying about Mae?"

"I said this in the last police report when Cyles disappeared. Mae had been talking like she knew something was wrong with him, kind of like he had gone crazy or something. He only laid a hand on little Donald once. Picked him up by the collar and scared him half to death! I told him, if he ever laid another hand on those babies, I would beat him with the same skillet I made dinner for him with when he was younger."

Clarence in the background. "She isn't afraid to use that skillet Detective."

"Shut up, Clarence. Anyways, Mae and I talked a lot about what was going on at that house. She said it was like things were moving around by themselves, and she would hear strange noises at night."

"What kind of noises, Ma'am?"

"Like someone was walking around outside the home or the floors would be squeaking and such."

"Did she ever talk about the children?"

"Of course! Those precious, poor, little angels." She began to tear up over the phone.

"Those two were my babies, I raised them with Mae for five years before Cyles returned home."

"You have my condolences for your loss Ma'am. I will do what I can to find out who did this."

"Thank you, Detective. But she said she had one run-in with Cyles when the kids were playing down in the basement again. He had snatched up little Donald and told him never to go down to the basement again."

"Did he hurt the child?"

"He said no when I came after him. The poor boy had three large scratch marks going down his back. He swore to Mae and me that Cyles didn't do it. He just drew him in by the collar to scare him from coming down to the basement because he had been building a preserve pantry for Mae, and he didn't want the kids getting hurt."

"Did you ever find out what caused the scratches?"

"No, they were gone within a day. The craziest thing, I tell yeah. I was about…" She cut out as a muffled argument could be heard over the phone. Then Clarence Deckler came back over the phone again.

"My wife put the fear of God in my nephew that day about how he handled the children, Sir. I think those poor kids didn't like Cyles to much after he got back from the war. He was a little rough around the edges if you ask me. My nephew is a good man detective. He had just gone through a lot over there in the war."

"I understand, I've seen this a lot in other cases dealing with war veterans."

"Please help our family detective."

"I will do my best, Sir. Is there anything else you remember that could help this case?"

"Oh! My wife and Mae used to talk about a diary she had made for Mae a little while ago too. She wrote in that thing every day,

I swear it."

"A diary? Where did she keep it?"

"Clarence, give me back the phone!" Anna proclaimed as I heard her take the phone back from him.

"Next to her bed somewhere in their bedroom detective. Clarence also told me about a box Cyles brought back with him. Cyles was very strict about other people touching it. Even went off on my husband about it once."

"Hmmm. Well, thank you so much for the information, Mr. and Mrs. Deckler. We will do everything we can to make sure whoever did this is caught. Now, unless there is any other information, I need to get back."

A short pause came from the other side of the phone, then some mumbling.

"That's its, Sir, thank you."

"Yes, Ma'am. I will call again if anything comes up. Bye."

I take the phone and hang it up as I hear multiple footsteps heading up the stairs to the second floor.

I leave the kitchen walking around through the living room and make my way up the stairs.

A diary. Could be useful to this investigation, maybe Mae kept track of what her husband did…

My thoughts disappeared from my mind as I witnessed the gruesome sight of the second floor. The second-floor hallway was smeared with bloody handprints, and there were even holes and scratches along the wall. I turned slightly to the left to see the blood trailed out of the last room of the house.

That must be the master bedroom.

My eyes followed the trail from the last room to where I was standing. There was one door on the left, a possible bathroom to the right, and one-bedroom almost directly in front of me. There were two cops in the last room facing away from me. A voice came from the bedroom closest to me.

"Barnes, in here."

I walked immediately into the first bedroom to see Officer Puller standing next to Doctor Oscar. The bedroom was dainty with dolls on shelves and a few stuffed animals here and there along with a twin-size bed.

"Who could do such a thing." I heard Puller say as he choked up.

Walking towards him, I got a glimpse of what he was referring too. A small girl laid sprawled on the floor. Her head was bashed open in the back as she soaked in a pool of her own blood.

"Bonnie Deckler, age eight, cause of death; open head injury due to blunt force trauma. Something slammed this poor girl against the edge of the metal striker on the door frame."

I turned to look at the door to see a large bloodstain with some strands of hair left on the striker part of the doorknob.

She must have fallen straight back on to the metal piece with a massive amount of force to cause a head injury as bad as the one she had sustained.

The sound of the doctor's camera flashing startled me out of my thoughts. I began to look around the small girl's bedroom, but I could not see anything else that would help me with this case. The room, besides the girl on the floor, was spotless as if someone had just cleaned it.

"Have you gone into the master bedroom yet?"

I turned to look at Puller as he was staring at me.

"No, I haven't. I had just made my way upstairs when I saw you and Doctor Oscar in here."

"It's pretty bad, Detective. The boy is in the master bedroom. The bathroom and the boy's bedroom are clean."

"Is this not bad enough?"

Doctor Oscar spoke up while checking his camera.

"The boy's name is Donald Deckler, between the ages of nine

and ten. The amount of trauma his body endured before he died is… well, its unimaginable to think a human could be capable of such an act."

"Coming from you, Doctor, it must be bad. Puller, you said a complete search was done on another bedroom and a bathroom?"

"Yes, they had just finished both rooms before informing us of the master bedroom. The Doctor and I walked in their earlier before starting on the girl here. I hope you don't have a queasy stomach Detective. I personally will not be setting foot in that room again."

I let out a sigh. "I am going to head to the master bedroom, Oscar. Let me know if you find anything else besides that one injury on her head."

"Will do Detective."

Leaving the girl's bedroom and heading down the hallway, a strong smell of blood filled the air, the closer I got to the master bedroom. The two police from earlier came walking out of the master bedroom, both looking sickly.

"God, I can't even imagine what that boy endured."

"I know right, it is unforgivable. We can't let whatever did this stay on the loose!"

The two continued with their conversation as I passed them.

A sense of dread came over me as I continued to walk towards the bedroom at the very end of the hallway.

CHAPTER 6
The Change

Journal Entry of Mae Deckler No. 3

Cyles has changed and in the worst way! The other day he made our poor son pee his pants, and my daughter is having nightmares about the incident that happened in the basement! There were scratch marks on Donald's back; also, I am so angry with him! How could he be so heartless to make his children never want to be around him again? Since our fight, he has been sleeping on the couch in the living room. His Aunt was over the other day, I told her about the basement incident. She struck him with her hand in front of me in the kitchen when she heard he had held Donald up by his collar. I was astonished to see her do it, but I was not upset about it. His Aunt is the bravest and strongest woman I know.

Anyways, the house has changed as well, like the whole atmosphere is

The Tale of Two

different. I tried to ignore it a first, but it has just gotten progressively worse. Things seem to move on their own. Or I hear noises at night… either from the first floor or the basement maybe? But when I make Cyles go check, he never finds anything. I don't even feel comfortable living in this house anymore. I am always on edge like something is watching me. Hopefully, I can figure out something for the kids and me soon.

I sprang awake as I sat up and looked around the darkroom. It was the living room, I could tell when my vision came too, and I was staring at the fireplace. Rubbing my eyes, everything was silent in the house. *Damn, I forgot I was sleeping on the couch now.* I let out a sigh lowering my head to my hands and running my fingers through my messy hair. *I hate sleeping on this damn thing, but Mae is still furious with me. But I don't even remember most of the incident like I was asleep or something.* A low growl came from outside the living room window, which made me turn quickly. My heart began to pound rapidly as I listened carefully, not sure if what I heard was correct. Suddenly a noise of slow clicks sounded from inside the kitchen. I quickly sat up and grabbed the nearest thing, the fireplace poker.

I snuck into the kitchen, holding the poker tightly with both hands. The clicking continued as I searched for the sound inside the kitchen, but the noise was just echoing. Continuing my search, I got to the back of the kitchen where the hallway was that led to the basement door and back into the living room. The noise was coming from the backdoor. I watched as the doorknob turned very slightly left then right and then back again. I squinted my eyes at the glass panel in the door to see what was outside, but I could not see anything. Raising the poker up to swing, I sauntered closer towards the door until it eventually stopped. Peering out the door's glass panel, all I could see was the kid's swing set and the forest behind that. For a short time, I stared until I saw a large shadow move swiftly across the yard and to the right of our home. It made me jump back as my heart jumped to my throat. I walked quickly through the hallway, back into the living room.

Looking from the living room towards the front door, I could not see anything out of the window. I began to sneak up on the door as I held the poker above my head, waiting for the intruder to attempt to enter my home. It seemed like I had been standing there for an eternity before I lowered my guard. *Maybe I am just sleep deprived and seeing things. It has been a while since I got a good night's sleep since I been forced to retire to the couch.* I shook my head and agreed with myself. *I just need to sleep.* Turning away from the door, I headed back for the sofa.

Then the front doorknob began to shake like the backdoor. This time I could feel eyes staring at me from behind. My heart raced as I began to turn slowly. Until I saw it through the glass panels of the door. The head of a ram with glowing yellow eyes. Its heavy breathing fogged the windows so I could not make out the entire thing. It was blacker than the night itself as the air around me became cold as ice. There I stood, paralyzed with fear as we stared into each other's eyes.

You have summoned me.

My mind screamed danger as my body began to move like it had its own free will. My hand, which was not my own anymore, grasped the doorknob. I could still feel it, it was colder than the room and air around me. I attempted to scream out for help, but no words came as I slowly turned the doorknob open and with an audible click. Letting go of the door and taking a step back, the door began to swing open gently by itself. The horned creature walked through the entryway as its hooves clicked on the wooden floors. No words could describe what I was seeing in front of me as it turned to look at me.

The head of a goat with a longer snout with short black fur, blood ran down from where its horns protruded from its head. A symbol carved into its very flesh on its forehead, its yellow eyes with horizontal pupils looked down upon me with intensity. The creature was much taller than I was with its goat-like legs and large arms. Its human-like hands had five fingers with pointed nails at the ends. The beast lifted his hand and made a sign with his fingers. Raising his middle and index finger while curling his ring and pinky finger and tucking in his thumb toward the palm of his hand. The creature let out a breath through its nostrils that were hot and smelled of sulfur.

Present your head Cyles.

My body began to convulse as I was forced to lean my head forward towards its hand. I fought with everything I had, but it was no use. The creature placed its two fingers upon my forehead and spoke in a language I could not comprehend. I fell to the floor once it finished speaking and removed its fingers. My body contorted painfully. Laying on the floor in agonizing pain, I watched helplessly as the creature slowly made its way out the front door as it felt like I was dying.

***

The sound of a door closing downstairs woke me up out of my sleep. I stared into the pitch-black ceiling of our bedroom as I wondered, *what the hell was that?* I listened carefully as I heard what sounded like stumbling coming from downstairs and maybe what sounded like kitchen drawers opening and closing. Anger began to rage inside of me. *Is he drunk!? As if he has not dug a deep enough hole already!* I threw back the covers violently and leaped out of bed. Stomping down the hallway, I made my way down the stairs as I heard another door open and close. The front door was closed as I turned the corner into the living room. He was not asleep on the couch. I pulled my nightgown tighter around me as anger built up inside of me.

Loud stomping came from the basement stairs as I quickly made my way to the basement door. I opened it to see that the stair light was off.

"Cyles! What are you doing? Do you have any idea what time it is?"

I huffed with anger as I reached to turn on the staircase light and began to make my way down slowly. Doing my best not to trip. I stopped dead as a low growl came from the basement.

"Cyles? What is that?"

Still no response. I changed my pace to creep down the stairs and peered around the corner of the staircase. The basement was completely dark as I peered around the corner. Making out just an outline of something standing in the middle of the basement.

"Cyles? What are you doing?"

The outline did not budge. Turning behind me to flip on the light switch, I turned back around to see Cyle's staring at the pantry on the other end of the basement. As I started to speak, I noticed his stance was off, and blood was trickling off his fingertips onto the floor as his arms were relaxed by his side. He held something in his right hand.

"Oh my god, Cyles! What have you done to yourself!"

Pure terror took control of my body when he turned around to face me. His eyes rolled back into his head as he bore a mark on his forehead that appeared to be something of a bruise that his veins protruded from. His cheek skin was deteriorating, showing his jawbones and bare teeth—the gums in some places were missing along with portions of his lips. Blood was leaking from the orifice that was his mouth and nostrils and had stained his shirt torso and sleeves. He held a kitchen knife in his right hand that was covered in blood. What was left of his lower face opened and closed as he attempted to breathe.

A low wet gurgle could be heard as he attempted to speak. "Ki…ll…me."

To traumatized by the horrific sight, I could not move, speak, or even think.

"Mae, kill… me. P-lease."

The pantry door burst open as another figure slowly appeared in its entryway. My whole body told me to run, but I was too petrified. A creature with an outline of horns and an animal's face appeared out of the darkness. It spoke in an unrecognizable language as Cyles made a bolt for the basement door. Aggressively, his gurgle became a yell of terror as he struggled to open the basement door.

Letting out a horrific scream my body was causing me to hold back, I turned and ran up the basement stairs as fast as I could. Reaching the top, I slammed the basement door shut and struggled to lock it from the violent shaking in my hands. I took off at a sprint racing to get around the living room and up the stairs. I stumbled at the top as I went through the first bedroom door snatching Bonnie out of her bed. Leaving her room as she was still half asleep and starting to realize something was wrong by asking me questions that I did not answer. I opened Donald's bedroom door and woke him up, telling him we are leaving the house now. He was dazed and confused by all the commotion but jumped up quickly once he saw how serious I was.

"Mom, what's wrong?"

"We are going to your Aunt and Uncle's house right now, baby. We have to hurry."

Once he was out of his bed, we took off out of his room and for the stairs. Bonnie's dead weight was taking a toll on my body as I carried her down the stairs at what felt like a sprint. Reaching the front door, I opened it as we all took off at a dash across the front yard towards the gravel road heading towards the Deckler residence. The cold night air hurt my lungs as I carried Bonnie in one arm and hurried Donald along with my other. My entire body ached as my mind played the events that had just taken place on repeat in my mind.

What was I going to tell them when we got to their house? That my husband had lost his mind and mutilated his own face with a kitchen knife. That there was a horrific creature in our preserve pantry? No, no one would believe me. They would take my children away from me. I would have to lie. I would have to tell them that my husband has gone missing, and we heard loud noises that woke me in the middle of the night that spooked me out of my sleep.

Little did I know that this would be the last time that I would ever see my husband Cyles.

CHAPTER 7
Mae's Diary

Reaching the master bedroom door, it was only open a crack. The smell of blood poured out of the room. Reaching for the doorknob and slowly opening the door, my heart skipped a beat once I got a clear view of the room. Blood covered almost every inch of the room: the furniture, the walls, the door, even some streaking on the ceiling. Upon closer inspection of the site, organic material could be seen in the blood splatter. It appeared as if the victim was beyond mutilated and torn apart by the assailant. The smell of the room was beyond overbearing. Pulling a handkerchief out of my back pocket, I used it to cover my mouth and nose as I gagged a little stepping into the room.

The Tale of Two

I had seen a few homicide cases since I have returned from the war, but nothing as gruesome and horrible as this young boy's death. Not even memories of bloodshed from the war could prepare me for this. Stepping carefully around the bedroom, doing my best not to contaminate the evidence with my shoe prints, with multiple awkward contortions and side steps, I had finally made it to the side of the bed. Still holding my handkerchief to my mouth and nose, I leaned over the bed to get a better few of the other side of the bed.

There he laid, just a few feet from the bed opposite of me. The body was to the point of unrecognizable; no face, barely any arms or legs, half his torso gone. Turning away quickly as my stomach turned on me, I felt as if my innards would be rejected from my body. *No human could have possibly done this, a carnivorous animal had attacked, mutilated, and devoured this boy before I guess being discovered. Usually, from what I read, large predatory mammals tend to waste not a meal because they would not know when the next one would come.*

Looking around the room behind me, I felt a warm afternoon breeze come through the broken bedroom window. Stepping carefully towards the window, I looked out and down at the yard. *Our assailant must have escaped through the window. Maybe after being discovered? Or a fight broke out up here?*

Turning my attention back towards the room, I saw that the nightstand to the right of me and the bedside drawer was cracked open. Reaching for it, I slid it open to see the contents inside. In the drawer laid a women's comb, mirror, some trinkets, and a small leather-bound book. Looking over the text that presented no title, I picked it up with my unoccupied hand to get a closer inspection. It was a notebook or journal of some kind with a leather strap that held the book closed. Undoing the belt delicately, I read the back of the front cover.

To Mae,

Here is a journal to write down all your favorite new memories once Cyles returns home from the war.

Love,

Anna Deckler

This is the diary that Anna spoke about over the phone earlier. I began to flip through the pages of the journal. There were different entries with different dates, all of them numbered in sequence. I began to read entry one through three. It was a slow progression of what appears to be Cyles' mental health degrading from the horrors of war until I got to entry number four.

Journal entry of Mae Deckler No. 4

Last night was one of the most terrifying and horrific nights of my life. Cyles has lost his mind… I found him in the basement, cutting his face with a butcher knife, along with someone or something else. Something I am too terrified to put into words on paper in this journal for fear if someone, where to find this journal, would think I was the insane one. I had escaped the home with Bonnie and Donald and made it to Clarence and Anna's house down the road. I told them as much as I could without sounding completely insane. We called the police and made a report over the phone line, and Clarence went to the house to try and find Cyles, but he said when he got their Cyles was nowhere to be found, and the basement doors leading to the outside were still intact. All that was left of him was his blood on the basement floor.

I continued to read as the ink was smeared with wet droplet stains towards the bottom of the page of entry four.

I don't know what to do anymore. I feel lost, and nothing makes sense. Cyles is gone again and possibly forever this time, to where no one knows, and I am raising our children by myself, again.

Entry number four ends with that last note.

I skimmed through the next few pages, every entry seems to be her having distrust within herself and doing her best to stay strong for the children who are more confused on the situation then she is. It continues with her dealings with the police and how no one still seems to have any idea where the mentally unstable Cyles has gone. Until I got to another entry in which she speaks of moving back into the house three weeks later.

Journal entry of Mae Deckler No. 7

Three weeks have gone by now, and there are still no whereabouts of where Cyles might be. The police have finished their investigation in the basement and the rest of the home. They even did their best to clean up for us before we moved back into the house today. It's so strange being back in this house, with everything that has happened. The children feel the same way I suspect from their actions. Ideas of selling the home and moving somewhere else have popped into my head here recently. I personally believe that I may never see Cyles again, not after what I witnessed that terrible night.

Journal entry of Mae Deckler No. 8

Bonnie came to my bed last night; said she had heard noises downstairs in the middle of the night that scared her awake. I went downstairs but did not hear a thing, but as I walked through the house, I did notice that the basement door was left ajar. Even though I do my best to avoid going down into the basement, I have witnessed the kids attempting to time to time. I closed the door without looking down the stairs and continued to search the rest of the house and found nothing. I let Bonnie sleep in the bed with me for the night.

Journal entry of Mae Deckler No. 9

Besides Bonnie having me on edge last night, I received a phone call from a detective from the local police department this morning asking me a lot of odd questions. Had my husband been part of any club or organization. Had I ever noticed anyone else in the basement beside the kids and Cyles, and did I know anything about a box in the basement. Of course, I told him no to the club and box question, but I was not entirely sure about him bringing anyone else into our basement. I had heard noises coming from downstairs at night a few times that I could not explain, and the night everything went wrong, I heard doors open and close. I told the detective everything I could remember about the noises I had heard and the doors opening and closing late at night, but I dared not tell him anything else for the sake of my children.

Journal entry of Mae Deckler No. 10

I gained enough courage to venture down to the basement today while the kids were playing on the swing set outside. Everything seemed to be intact except everything was clean and without a speck of dust. I went into the pantry Cyles had been working on and found the box the detective mentioned. It was sitting on a long wooden table that Cyles must have built. Their where half-melted candles and what appeared to be woven grass or hay and animal bones. Among this odd collection was a strange mahogany box. It had a language carved into the top that I could not understand, and besides an antiqued brass clasp on the front, the sides were sealed with red wax.

The strangest part of the box is when I went to pick it up, and I began to feel as if something was watching my every move in the basement. Once I exited the pantry is when things got weird. I swear I heard a voice speak to me, very softly but a voice I am sure of it. It spooked me so bad I ran carrying the box up the stairs as fast as I could and slammed the basement door behind me. I hid the box under my bed for now until I could figure out what to do with it.

I puzzled at entry number ten as I placed my thumb in the middle of entries nine and ten and closed the journal. I peered at the blood-stained bed and begin to slowly lift the blanket and sheets that draped over the side of the bed, I bent down and peered underneath the bed: nothing but an empty floor with some blood splatter that manages to seep underneath.

Where would Mae have taken the box, and why did that previous detective want to know more about the table? Maybe he thought he was part of a cult or was into the occult?

I opened the journal and began skimming through the next few entries, looking for any clues of what might have happened to the box. As I continued to look through the logs, number 13 caught my attention.

Journal entry of Mae Deckler No. 13

Ever since I brought the box up from the basement, I have had a strange fascination with it. I… I hear voices that tell me things, but I am sure if it's just me talking to myself in my head? Also, things seem to move around inside the house. Like, the couch was a foot closer to the fireplace. I think I might even be seeing things, too; the other day, I swear I saw a shadow figure move from the living room into the hallway.

I must know what's inside this box… why it's the only thing I can ever think about here lately. It also might contain the answers to what happened to Cyles that night.

Journal entry of Mae Deckler No.14

I am having trouble sleeping at night. I feel as if things are… watching me, and I am having nightmares about that thing I think I saw that night when I found Cyles. Things have also gotten much stranger, I hear movement outside the house at night too, but every time I check out the windows, I see nothing. I don't know what's going on anymore. I feel as if all this torment will stop if I just open that damn box. The children don't even seem to notice anything, besides their father has been missing for some time now. They are not hearing or seeing anything that I have been for the past few days since I came across this box.

I just don't think I can take this torture anymore; I plan to open the box tomorrow. I need to know what happened to Cyles and what's currently going on with me right now.

I turn the next page to see that Mae's writing style has become more frantic.

Journal entry of Mae Deckler No. 15

Opening the box was a mistake... we need to leave this house now! Before it comes. It will come back for me, I am sure of it! Like it did for Cyles! I need to leave. I need to pack up the kids and leave. But where can we go? Where can we stay now that I know! Now that, it knows...

I flip to the next page to see that its blank. I thumb ahead a few more pages to see that this apparently was the last entry that Mae Deckler ever made in her journal. I flipped back a few pages until I got to entry number 15 again and saw that the date of the entry was the same date that the family was murdered.

A muffled scream came from downstairs that startled me out of my thoughts and made my heart jump. Without thinking, I dropped the journal and took off at a sprint towards the stairs that led down to the first floor. Doctor Oscar and Officer Puller were already shuffling quickly down the stairs once I began my descent. After maneuvering down the stairs as fast as possible, we heard the scream again.

"Oscar. Head outside with Officer Miller, tell any remaining officers outside that we have a situation."

He frantically shook his head once and took off out the front door.

"Puller, come with me."

We both drew our pistols from our holsters and moved our way tactically into the kitchen. As we turned the corner out of the kitchen and into the small hallway, we saw Sheriff Jones and a fellow officer attempting to break the basement door down. Sheriff Jones turned to look in our direction; the look on his face was severe.

"Puller, detective, give us a hand, why don't you! Something has Officer Hanes in the basement!"

"Step back!"

We all moved away from the door as Puller pointed his .38 special revolver at the locking mechanism between the door and wall frame. With a loud bang and some splintering, the door flung open inwards as we all made a dash one by one through the basement entryway down the stairs. Officer Puller took his flashlight out of his belt and pointed it towards the end of the stairs, while the sheriff attempted to turn on the basement light.

The Tale of Two

"The lights dead."

We all pulled out flashlights as we made it to the bottom of the stairs with guns drawn and lights filling the room.

"Hanes! Where are you?"

The basement is silent, but a stench of rot fills the area. We began to slowly fan out and search the cellar until the police officer with the sheriff speaks up.

"Detective! I found something, it looks like a box."

I slowly move forward towards his direction with my gun drawn as I see where his flashlight is pointed at. It's a mahogany box that is on its side with its contents spilled out onto the concrete floor. I bend down to take a closer look going over each object with my light. A small brass goblet, a carving that appears to be made of bone, hair tied together with some string, a dead rose, and a broken used candle with a holder. Puller slowly made his way past me as I looked over the objects.

"HELP ME! ARGGHHHH!"

"Hanes! He is in the closet!" Puller yells as the two police officers run towards the closed door.

I stand quickly and draw my pistol down on the pantry along with the sheriff as Puller begins to open the door. As the door opens, Puller appears to have frozen solid.

"Puller! Puller, what is it?"

Metal hitting the concrete floor can be heard as his gun falls. His arms fall limp at his side as his feet slowly left the ground. He is lifted and moved out of the way of the door. As he gargles blood in pain and attempts to scream. A large silhouette of a creature becomes visible as Puller's body is moved slowly away from the pantry door frame.

"Holy shit! Puller!"

The police officer to the right of Puller immediately starts firing off rounds into the creature as we join in. It lets out a horrific screech. Puller's body falls to the floor as the lights of our flashlights reveal the true nature of the shadow.

A decrepit creature that appears to be what's left of a human stands before us. Skin taut over bones, grey with the stench of rot. A face that matches the description of a human, but the bottom jaw is missing with a long unnatural tongue that hangs and wriggles as the thing screeches. Its knees are bent in the opposite direction like a dog, and its arms are elongated. Its hands are black, and its fingers are bones with sharp pointed edges. Blood drips from them as it raises one hand and moves with such quickness and strikes the police officer standing in front of us with such force it sends him into the concrete wall with a loud crunch.

The sheriff and I continue firing at the thing as it turns to look at us. It roars while protruding its head towards us, it raises its hand again to strike. Our bullets make an impact with its torso as it staggers backward, attempting to stay on its feet. Within a second, the horrid thing turns and lunges for the basement door to the outside. With a loud crash, it runs through the metal door and out of the basement. I run towards the opening to see that it is sprinting across the field with what appears to be limp. I fire off two more shots at the creature, winging it in its left shoulder, sending it staggering forward. My 1911 reports with a loud click, locking the slide to the rear. I am out of rounds.

"Detective!"

I turn to see Sheriff Jones huddled over Puller's body, placing two fingers on his neck.

"He's still alive, but bleeding out! We gotta radio in for paramedics!"

Puller gargles and coughs up blood as he tries to speak.

"I am not gonna make it sheriff. Tell… tell Monica that I love her… and that we raised a fine young boy. That… that I am sorry, I am not gonna make it home for supper…"

Tears began to stream down his face as he grabbed the sheriff's hand.

"Tell them both that they made me the happiest man alive."

With his last words, his hand went limp in sheriff's.

Jones placed Puller's hand on his chest as a tear fell onto Puller's uniform.

"What the fuck was that thing, Detective?"

"From what I found inside the house, I believe it's what's left of Cyles Deckler."

"What the hell do you mean, what's left?"

I began to explain all the evidence I have found inside, including the journal and the box and how it drove both Cyles and Mae mad. How Mae found Deckler in the basement and so on.

He paused, looking at me with great astonishment before his face returned to normal and then became angered.

"I want a search party for that fucking thing! Now! We will fan out with the dogs and cover the whole side of Doolittle Hill forest. He is injured and will probably be dead by the time we find him, and if not, he will wish he was."

He stood up and took his hat off and ran his fingers through his hair as he walked out of the basement and into the backyard. I turned to look at Puller again as he lay in a pool of his own blood. His injuries matched the wife and son inside the house. I took my fedora off my head as I turned to look at the other police officer. Also, dead. The creature had thrown him so hard into the basement wall that it killed him on impact.

I turned and made my way to the pantry door and peered inside. The only thing inside was some blood splatter and the table with the weird trinkets that Mae described in her journal. *Where the hell is Officer Hanes? Shouldn't his body be here like the rest of the victims?* Looking around the small pantry for clues, I had found my answer. A small window near the ceiling used to bring in natural light had been smashed out. *He must have escaped through the opening during the fight, but where is he now? I need to report this to the sheriff as soon as possible.*

I walked out of the basement and into the backyard to see a small blood trail that leads off into the forest. The same direction the creature ran when I shot it in the back shoulder. We would hunt Cyles Deckler down before the day became night.

CHAPTER 8

Man Hunt

It did not take long after Sheriff Jones's call before police reinforcements along with dogs showed up at the River Side Roadhouse to form a search party. We all circled around in the front yard as Sheriff Jones began to speak.

"Listen up, yawl! After gathering evidence in the house and speaking with Detective Barnes and Coroner Oscar, we are led to believe the man we are hunting down this afternoon is Cyles Deckler. He has murdered his wife, his two children, and two of our own that we know of so far. Officer Hanes is still MIA as of right now. His appearance has been mutilated, he will be missing his bottom jaw, and his skin is greyish in color as strange as that sounds. Cyles is severely injured and has been shot multiple times. This leads me to believe he has not gotten far. As of right now, those are all the details we have on him. This man is perilous and should be treated with extreme prejudice if found."

Standing by Sheriff Jones' side, I looked out upon the crowd as they began to mumble at his statement and converse among themselves as the Sheriff paused to look over the crowd's reaction.

"Our base of operation will be the back yard of this home. We will form into three-man hunting parties, and everyone will have a radio. I want a dog in every group, if possible. I want everyone to fan out as far as possible and search every acre of this forest. If found, radio the base of operations with your location. We have marked where Cyles' blood trail begins and have some of his clothes out back for your dogs to catch his scent. Let's hunt this bastard down!"

The crowd's mumbling grew to everyone talking at once as they all headed around the back of the house.

"Detective."

I turned to look at Sheriff Jones.

"I want you and Miller to come with me. I'll get my hound dog, Cooter."

"Okay, Sheriff, just let me check on one more thing."

"Sure, but don't take too long. We ain't got enough daylight left."

As Sheriff Jones and Officer Miller began to walk off towards the many vehicles in the driveway where other police officers were getting the dogs ready. I took off for the back of the house. The words of Mae's Journal rang through my head as I thought about that box I found earlier in the basement. *How could a box cause all of this?* As I continued to walk towards the shelter doors that led into the basement. I watched as much of the search party prepared for the hunt; gathering radios and flashlights, loading firearms, and separating into teams of three.

I stepped down into the basement entrance, doing my best to avoid the broken metal door that the creature had run through earlier to see that the box from earlier was still in the middle of the basement floor. As I turned on my flashlight and pointed it at the box, it was different than I recalled. Taking a closer look as I slowly made my way across the basement towards it, the box was no longer open or laying on its side. The contents of the box had also disappeared. Studying the box, I slowly reached down and picked it up.

Like a flash of lightning, a horrifying image popped into my head. A creature with yellow eyes, horns, and a face that resembled a goat appeared. I fumbled the box, almost dropping it from being startled. *What the hell was that?* I looked around the room to make sure I was still sane—nothing but me and an empty basement. Looking the box over as I held it, I could see where the wax seal has been broken on the sides. The latch was the only thing holding the box closed. Without hesitation, almost as if I was forced, I unhinged the latch and opened the box.

Darkness, darker than anything I had ever witnessed, engulfed the room as the air grew thin and cold, I could feel my breath escape from me, almost as if I was choking. Fear gripped my body as I froze in my current position. I could sense a second presence as it entered the room.

A low unnatural voice spoke to me from all around the room. "Barnes Ramirez."

Against my own will, my body turned to face a creature that stood now directly in front of me. A goat's head with massive horns that have been forced through its skull since blood ran down its face. Its piercing yellow eyes starred into the very depths of my soul. As it spoke to me again, the heat that escaped from its body was almost unbearable as the smell of sulfur filled the room.

"I see the unyielding hunger that resides inside you."

My body began to forcefully hold out my left arm as it raised its hand, making a sign with its fingers. Placing two fingers upon my left wrist, it spoke in a language I could not comprehend. The veins in my wrist turned black with its touch, and pain took over as I began to scream. A scar appeared on my wrist, a circle with a Z running through the middle of it.

Within an instant, it felt like I woke up from a terrible nightmare. I looked around the basement, everything was normal. I looked down at my left wrist, but there was nothing there. *Had it been a delusional dream? A vision of some kind.* I looked down to see that the box sat untouched and closed. As I stared at it, a voice spoke inside my head in an incomprehensible language. Immediately, a pain shot through my left arm that made me clinch.

"Arghh. Damn!"

A noise came from the basement shelter door entrance. A dog let out a loud echoing bark into the basement.

"Detective? Is that you down there?"

The pain subsided in an instant, and when I looked at my arm, all that was left was the black mark from what I thought was a vision. I unrolled my sleeves as fast as I could to cover up the brand. "Yes… yes, it's me. How did you know I was down here?"

The sheriff poked his head around the entrance looking around till his eyes focused on the box and then me.

"Some of the officers told me they saw you come down here. What you doing?"

I paused for a second to get my story straight. "I… I was just having another look around, wanted to make sure I did not miss anything."

"You can do that later. We got a killer to hunt down."

"Your right, let's get going."

As I walked out of the basement and back into the backyard, I was greeted by a large brown bloodhound that the sheriff called Cooter. He smelled me as he wagged his tail for a few seconds and then went back to focusing on everyone else around him. As the sheriff and I headed towards the backyard, we were calling the "command center" Miller came from around the front of the house towards us.

"I heard about what happened in the basement Sheriff, how unfortunate. This Deckler prick just became one of the most hated cop killers in the state of Indiana."

"He won't live past tonight, Miller. Well enough chit chat, let's get a move on. Miller, you grab a radio and two flashlights for our team and Detective you might want to reload your pistol and grab a 12 gauge."

Miller and I both nodded our heads and left to grab what we needed before the search. We met back up with the sheriff as he was letting Cooter get a good sniff of Deckler's blood and some of his old clothes. The dog began sniffing the ground and then started pulling Sheriff in the direction of the woods.

"You got the scent, boy? Let's go get him."

Cooter led our party of three, deep into the woods as he

followed Deckler's scent intensely. After about two hours of searching, a howl rang throughout the woods to the right of our location. We all immediately turned to that direction and searched through the woods with our eyes. The radio let out an auditable static noise before a voice came through.

"This is Officer Mason. We found Officer Hanes on an uphill climb northeast of where everyone entered the woods from the Deckler's residence, he's gone, over."

Miller put the radio close to his face and pushed the button.

"This is Officer Miller. We are west of your position and coming to you, over."

Sheriff tugged on Cooter's leash as we lead him off his scent path towards the direction of the dog bark. We hiked through the woods as it became steeper with the hill, and the sun just began to start setting. Cooter suddenly refused to walk on any further.

"Come on, boy, we gotta go." Said the Sheriff as he pulled on Cooter's leash, but the dog would not budge.

Miller stopped walking to turn and look at the hound dog. "What's wrong with your dog, Sheriff?"

"I don't know. Cooter usually doesn't act like this."

A loud howl close to our location broke the silence of the woods and some muffled yelling.

"Miller radio to see if they found him."

"Officer Mason, this is Miller over. Did you find Cyles Deckler, over?"

I looked down at Cooter to see his hair on the back of his neck was now standing up. He had taken an aggressive stance towards the direction of the uproar. Static from the radio came twice but no answer. Cooter's position shifted as he began to bark aggressively. The sheriff looked shocked when he looked down at his dog and towards the woods in front of him. He then turned to look at Miller and me.

"Somethings wrong… Cooter never gets this aggressive, unless…"

Suddenly gunshots could be heard in front of us. They were close.

"Shit! Come on! We need to get to their location and now!"

The sheriff bent down and let Cooter off his leash, and the dog took off at a sprint towards the location, and we followed behind him as closely as possible. The climb was challenging, and we began to lose sight of Cooter as he howled through the woods and sprinted towards the direction of the gunshots. Eventually, we came to a full clearing in the woods with a few trees.

"COOTER! Where you at boy?!"

Miller and I looked around for a brown dog to come running through the woods, but no dog came. The clearing had a single path that ran through it, headed north of our direction and south back towards the course of the house.

"Where the hell are we? And where did this path come from?"

"It's a deer path Miller, you would not have seen it so easily near the house. Radio them again."

I looked down the northside of the path as they waited on someone to contact us back through the radio. I followed the trail with my eyes till it made a slight right turn by a big tree headed up the broad hillside. When I saw something move quickly out of the corner of my eye by the large tree. I held up the shotgun towards the direction of the movement.

"Down there. I saw movement."

The sheriff and Miller turned to look in my direction and down the path. They both unholstered their pistols.

"Are you sure Detective?"

"Positive. Down by that large tree. It took off around the bend heading up the hillside once I looked at it."

"It could've been the dog, let's go."

As we began to hurry down the path, a loud screech echoed

through the woods, making my skin crawl.

"What the fuck was that?"

"I have a feeling that its Deckler."

Tree limbs could be heard snapping ahead of us on the path as we stopped moving to get a better listen. Suddenly the snapping became someone running, and it sounded like it was headed directly for us.

"Mason! Is that you?"

No answer came as the noise continued to grow louder until we caught a glimpse of a uniformed officer making his way down the path towards us. The screech came again as another speck could be seen chasing him from behind.

"Oh shit! I think that is Deckler!"

"HEELLPPP ME!"

The officer fell 50 yards in front of us as if he tripped. Cyles Deckler stood on top of him and began to slash his back with his elongated fingers and tore his uniform to shreds until blood began to show with every slash.

Immediately the sheriff and Miller unholstered their weapons and began to fire upon Deckler as they slowly moved closer to him. I held up my shotgun and pumped it once to load the empty barrel when the pain took over. The pain shot down my arm, and I almost dropped my gun in shock.

Barnes, kill them.

I held up the shotgun again with my left arm as the throbbing continued and pointed it directly at Miller's back. Unrelenting fear filled my body as I tried to fight it. I heard the safety click as I continued to resist being forced to look down the barrel of the shotgun at the front bead sight. I strained with all my might mentally and physically, but it was not enough. The gun went off with a loud bang as Miller was slammed face forward into the ground.

Oh my god! What have I done!

The Sheriff immediately turned in confusion to look at Miller, who was now face down on the path. His police coat shredded in the back and smoking from the buckshot. With a face of astonishment, he looked up at me in confusion.

"Sheriff! I don't know what happened! I just…"

Immediately Sheriff Jones hit the ground as Deckler attacked him. I pointed the shotgun at Deckler and pulled the trigger, and the gun made an audible click. It was empty. I hurried and pumped the shotgun as my hands shook. I pointed the gun in the direction of Cyles, but when I looked back up. Cyles had picked up the Sheriff and placed him over his shoulder like he weighed nothing and was running for the tree line on the edge of the path.

"NO!"

The shotgun went off with a loud boom as the pellets peppered a tree in front of Cyles. He was gone, and so was the Sheriff. I looked back at Miller, who was still lying face down on the ground. Is body laid sprawled out, and he did not move. I slowly walked towards Miller as realization set in on what I had done. I bent down next to him and gave him a slight push with my right hand. He was gone, I had killed him. As my guilt swelled up inside of me, I felt a single tear stream down my face.

I dropped the shotgun and fell to the ground on my knees. Almost losing myself in self-pity when a prickling feeling could be felt in my left arm. I immediately looked down at my sleeve and unbuttoned it slowly, I could see that my veins had turned a black and blue color. I continued to watch as a symbol appeared once again on my wrist. *What the hell is happening to me? Am I not me anymore?* Gentilly touching the symbol with a finger sent the sharp pain down my arm again, which made me flinch in pain.

Barnes, pursue them.

I looked around me as the voice spoke to me again, but no one was there. I stood up as the pain subsided in my arm and heard a branch break behind me. Turning quickly, I caught a glimpse of what might have been a shadow moving into the thicket off the side of the path. Again, the same noise could be heard down the way that led deeper into the woods. I turned to look back but saw nothing this time. That's when I noticed that darkness was creeping through the woods as the sun began to set. I bent down and picked up the flashlight that Miller had dropped when I shot him. I pointed the flashlight down the path that leads deeper into the dark woods, which filled me with this burning suspicion that if I did not save Sheriff Jones before nightfall, I would not make it out of these woods alive.

CHAPTER 9

Insanity

I continued down the path until it led me to a creek that gently cascaded over some rocks from an uphill climb. I pointed my flashlight at the stream, and then around my surroundings, darkness had begun to engulf the forest. As I looked around, I noticed I was lost in the woods at this point with no way of knowing my way out, except for the path that led me here in the first place and the creek, possibly, if I followed it downstream. There were two steep hillsides on either side of the stream, too steep to climb.

    I looked around for clues to where I might find the direction that Deckler took off in with Jones, but I saw nothing. As my thoughts began to drift into despair in my own head, my arm began to tingle with a numbing sensation again and gradually changed to pain. A headache shot across my temples as I held my hands to them.

Alone. Desperate… Killer.

I clenched my eyes shut and held my head tight with both hands as the words echoed. Until another voice spoke.

"Barnes?"

I immediately looked up to see what appeared to be Officer Miller standing in front of me. My mouth dropped as I glanced him over. A basketball-size hole was in his torso to where you could see some of his organs. I began to weep as guilt washed over me like a tidal wave.

"Miller… how? I… I shot you! I shot you in the back! You died!"

His facial gesture did not change as he continued to stare at me with no emotion.

"Climb the creek, or more blood will be spilled, if not. The fault will be yours."

He turned to point his finger up the creek. As he turned, he revealed the back of his tattered police uniform, peppered with buckshot, from where I had shot him.

"I am… am sorry, Miller! This is all my fault!"

Warm tears streamed down my face as I closed my eyes.

"It…" I opened my eyes again to see that he was no longer standing in front of me.

Frantically I spun around with the flashlight looking in every direction for Officer Miller, but there was no one except me and the oncoming darkness. *Was that real? Am I imagining things?* The pain in my arm resided again, like before, as I let out a deep sigh. *How much longer will you have to endure this pain? What does that creature want with me?*

"AHHHHH!" A yell heard from up the creek broke the silence. *That sounds like Jones! I must hurry.*

Running up the creek bed, I gripped my flashlight tightly. It seemed as if I was running faster than I have ever done before, but the higher the slope got, the more difficult the climb became. Eventually, I had to heave my body up and over large rocks that the creek cascaded off of. Every stone I scaled, the more dangerous the next climb became.

Pulling myself over the most massive rock yet, my arm began to burn fiercely. I almost let go during my climb the pain hurt so bad. I sat in the creek with water-soaked clothes, I didn't even notice because of the pain. As I looked down at my left arm, the mark from the basement had appeared once again.

Murderer, Killer… Monster.

"NO!" I yelled out loud.

"It's not my fault! I cannot control it!"

You can't undo what's already been done.

My heart jumped into my throat as I recognized the voice.

Let the hunger consume you, succumb to your desires.

As the words were spoken, my mouth began to salivate. My senses began to intensify, pain shot throughout my body as I fell over into the creek. The cold creek water washed over my body, giving me short breaks from the pain I was enduring until the pain stopped entirely. I pushed myself up out of the water as the chilled evening air hit my body and made me shiver. My head was throbbing as I looked to see my flashlight underwater a few feet in front of me. Still working, its light shined up the creek through the water.

As I followed the light with my eyes, I saw a silhouette of a towering figure a few feet in front of me in the wood line that ran alongside the creek. I reached for the flashlight quickly and pointed it directly at the wood line, but nothing was there. As I continued to look around, I noticed that the sun had almost set. Its red hue shined through the forest. A sense of panic came over me as I realized the inevitable. The night would be upon me soon.

My gut ached with a horrid feeling. *There is something wrong with these woods. Nothing feels right, I am in an entirely new area of its own.* Standing up quickly, I shivered from the cold night breeze that flowed through the forest. *I have to find Jones and quick!*

As I continued to walk through the creek, I heard branches breaking and leaves from past autumns shuffle from movement within the tree line that lined both sides of the stream. The slopes are too steep for any animal to move stealthily, but my paranoia grew.

The trees began to change the further I ventured into this new area. They became twisted and bare; the brush was mostly barbed with prickers. The whole aura of the woods seemed to change; the smell, look, and feel was completely different than when I entered earlier. It was like the forest itself was slightly trembling, but I was not sure if it was all in my head or not. So, I continued on, hurrying as fast as I could through the creek while occasionally pointing my flashlight to the left and right of me as my paranoia grew.

CHAPTER 10
Ritual

"SOMEONE HELP MEEE!"

    I was now sprinting through the woods as fast as I could towards the direction of the screaming. My flashlight had died from possible water damage minutes ago, a mysterious fire's light was the only thing that helped me see my way through the dark woods. Its glow revealed the end of the creek, a large vertical rock wall stood proud as the fire's lights touched every piece of it. As I got closer, a cave appeared on the wall. I could see dark silhouettes standing in a clearing in front of the cave as the horrid screaming continued.

    I came to a halt a few feet before I had reached the tree line that was the entrance of the clearing. I hid amongst the shadows of the tree line as the horrifying events came into view from a bonfire that burned in the right-side corner. A large flat rock laid in the middle over top of the creek that ran out of the cave, many creatures, maybe six stayed at bay from the stone on the edges of the tree line that made up the clearing. They were more massive than the average man, and they stood on all fours with a hunch in their backs that revealed the bones of their spine. They all had skulls for heads, and some even had antlers. Their red eyes reflected the light of the fire in the dark as they menacingly stared at it. Their skin was grey and stretched tight over their large boney figures, their hands resembled claws of large predatory animals.

In the middle of the clearing behind the large rock stood a beast darker than the night itself. Black smoked flowed off the creature like a long cloak as if it was burning alive. Its head resembled that of a ram, with bright yellow eyes and black vertical pupils and a symbol carved into its forehead. Large horns protruded out of his head, and it seemed to bleed from every orifice of its body, but it did not seem to feel pain. Its chest was bear and resembled something of a female human, but the rest of its body was covered in hair. It spoke in a language I could not understand, but as it spoke, something on top of the rock began to move and scream in misery.

It was Sheriff Jones! His body had been cut up, and part of his right leg was gone. His blood flowed off the rock and into the creek. The creatures formed around the beast, and the sheriff, howled an unearthly hollow noise as the beast spoke while holding its human-like hands over the top of Jones. My heart raced as my mind went through different scenarios of what I should do. The beating was so loud I was afraid the entire woods would hear it.

Suddenly realization struck me. *The beast that I had thought to be a vision that placed this mark upon my wrist was real! There it stood, directly in front of me torturing Sheriff Jones. I have to do something and fast!* I dropped the shotgun earlier next to Miller's body and discarded the broken flashlight a while back. Then I remembered *my pistol!* I looked down at my side where my holster would be, and there it was! Still clinging to my body by my leather shoulder holster.

Slowly I unholstered my pistol, making as little noise as possible. A roar came from the beast that almost made me jump. The creatures began to shuffle and howl as something else came from the tree line. It was Cyles Deckler! His skin resembled that of the creatures but with a mutilated human face. His abnormally long tongue swung as he staggered out into the clearing where the beast stood behind Jones. His spine was starting to protrude from his back, and his eyes looked glassed as if he were blind. He appeared injured from all the gunshot wounds he had endured from earlier. He stopped directly in front of the beast and blocked my view of Jones. The beast slowly raised his hand while pointing a finger directly at Cyles. It spoke once again and then looked at Jones. Cyles lunged at Jones and began to eat what was left of his right leg. The sheriff screamed in agony as Cyles attempted to devour him in front of the beast.

Without thinking, I stepped out of my hiding spot, pointing my gun at Cyles and the beast.

"ENOUGH! LEAVE HIM ALONE!"

The gatherings' attention turned towards me in a blink of an eye. Even Cyles' demented face had turned back to look at me as I shouted. The creatures began to screech so loud I had to cover one ear with my free hand before going entirely deaf. The beast raised its hands, and the creatures immediately stopped, even the thing that use to be Cyles began to hunch and slowly back away from Jones.

Slowly walking forward, the gun now pointed at the leader of this demonic cult.

"ALL OF YOU! GET BACK, NOW!"

The beast slowly lowered its hands as I began to advance towards it.

"Barnes?! *gasp* Is that you!?"

"It's me, Jones. Stay calm, I am going to get you out of here."

"No! You have to run! You don't understand what you're up against!"

My heart was now beating so fast that it hurt the inside of my chest. *What am I doing? What am I up against!*

"Listen, Barnes! *gasp* You must get away from here! Now!"

The beast began to raise one hand gently towards me and slowly pointed its finger as it spoke in another language. My body immediately froze without warning. I could not move any part of it. As the beast let its hand fall naturally, so did my pistol in front of me.

"BARNES… NO!"

My left arm became engulfed in pain as I fell before the beast. Rolling alongside the creek in agony, I screamed at the top of my lungs. The beast spoke again as one of the creatures made its way slowly towards me. I watched in pain as it salivated from must have been in its mouth. Its red eyes and black pupils fixed upon my helpless body. As the pain in my arm began to subside a little, I did my best to crawl forward towards Jones.

The creature had finally reached me. Its clawed hand reached for my leg as I reached nervously out in front of me for anything. Its claws sunk deep into my leg as I yelled in agony, still frantically reaching, clawing at the sandy, rocky banks of the creek. Until I grabbed it. The creature began to gently lift me up as its mouth opened, and its saliva poured onto my leg. When it turned me over, I stretched my arm as far forward as I could and placed the pistol directly into its mouth and pulled the trigger. With a thunderous boom, the creature staggered backward, dragging me with it, eventually releasing its claws from the innards of my leg.

It let out a deafening screech as I aimed the pistol again and fired off another round into its skull for a head. The thing immediately dropped, and all the breath it had left in its body escaped out its mouth with a putrid smell that would have caused me to gag, but the pain was too intense. I pushed myself away from it with all my upper body strength and sat up off the ground. Immediately turning to face the beast, I pointed my gun at it and pulled the trigger twice.

In a blink, another creature guarded the beast against those two rounds and collapsed to the ground. A screech sounded to the right of me as another creature came at me. I turned the gun slightly and fired off a round at the other creature, hitting it directly in the throat as it gargled and fell to the ground. As soon as its head hit the ground, I pulled the trigger again, sending another round into its skull. Its skull began to crack around the hole the bullet made.

As I turned to the next closest creature, a pain shot through my right shoulder blade and into my collar bone. My entire right arm dropped to the ground against my will. As I looked down at my right collar, five long claws protruded out of my torso covered in my blood. My head went limp as I began to cough up my own blood.

With all my strength I had left, I looked back up at the beast as it was now walking silently towards me, leaving a black smoke trail behind it. My neck went relaxed again, as my strength weakened. Looking at the ground, I noticed I was sitting next to the creek. My blood ran off the protruding claws onto the ground and into the stream ever so gently. My hands laid limp on the ground as well, pistol still in my right hand. The beast had hoofs for feet as it stepped within my limited view. My left arm began to lift on its own as the beast caught it with its right hand. It pressed its thumb into the mark it had placed on me as I screamed from the pain it produced. My veins started to slowly turn black from its touch and spiderweb outwards.

It made a hand gesture with its free hand and began to speak in that language once again. The creature behind me removed its claws with ease as more blood flowed from the holes that were left. With the two fingers that were raised still while making the gesture, it placed them upon my head. My body began to convulse as I fell to the ground, but it continued to hold me by my left arm. Its thumb still pressed into the mark on my wrist began to sink into my arm. My vision began to fade as I could only stare at its hoofs. I watched as the darkness of the woods around us engulfed us. I fought my hardest to stay conscious, but I was overwhelmed.

CHAPTER 11
A Vision

Snow blankets an abandoned light blue family home and sparkles in the night as a police patrol car turns into what is left of a snow-covered driveway. Its lights moving across the home, slowly illuminating the whole scene. The car's engine shuts off, but the headlights stay on as two police officers step out of the vehicle. Both producing flashlights from inside the vehicle began to light up the woods around them as they scan the area.

"Let's hurry and get this over with. This house gives me the creeps."

"It's not like the fucking house is haunted, Mick. We are just looking for signs of trespassing."

"Did you not hear about what happened here? A guy came home from the war and butchered his whole family in this house, kids and all! It was all over the news. Then a massive shoot out took place between the guy and the cops that showed up on the scene. Six cops killed, and a Sheriff and a Detective went missing! I used to know the Detective, we worked over in Louisville together for a little bit."

"No shit Mick. Everyone in this area knows about the Deckler family massacre. But that was almost a decade ago. Let's just search the property, make a report, and get back out on patrol. And would you please stop with the history lesson."

"I still don't like it! It feels almost as if we are not supposed to be here, Ben. Some even say that the woods around these parts are cursed."

"Would you shut the hell up! Stop being a damn chicken and do your damn job! We are just responding to do a trespassing report, that's it! Just search around the house for any footprints or any signs of attempted break-ins to the house. Now, I am going to search the right side of the home, and you are going to take the left side, copy? Yell out if you find any evidence or see someone."

"I still don't think this is a good idea."

"It doesn't matter what you think. Now get going."

Mick watched as Ben began to walk through the snow

towards the right side of the boarded-up home. One hand on a flashlight and one hand resting on his pistol in his waist holster. Mick shook his head and began to look around on the left side of the front yard for any clues.

Looking at the house, it had been long abandoned. All the windows and entryways were boarded up, and no vehicle sat in the carport. Shining a light in the house, there were no signs of a break-in. It was a quiet night, unlike last night's snowstorm and strong icy winds. The temperature outside was still well below freezing as Mick continues to walk around the side of the house through the carport.

At the back of the house, he points his light out towards the forest. A rusted and broken swing set barely stands covered in snow. Most of the backyard is a tall brush blanketed in snow. Scanning the yard with his flashlight, rustling can be heard to his right.

"Who's there!?" Mick yells, turning quickly, pointing his flashlight along the backside of the house. A shadow darts into a small opening behind the house that resembles what is left of the basement's cellar doors. Shining his light back at the ground where the shadow was, he sees no trace of footprints in the snow. Steadily walking closer towards what was left of the cellar doors, he shined his light down into the basement to see that the board that once closed off the basement was now smashed open.

"Hey, Ben! You might want to look…" A horrific yell cut him off. The screaming was coming from around the side of the house that Ben was investigating.

"BEN!"

Mick takes off at a sprint around the house to see a broad outline of someone standing over Ben. Drawing his gun at the silhouette, he holds up his flashlight to reveal the horror that stands before him. It was a large creature with taunt grey skin. Its head appeared to be a skull of a stag, and its humanoid hands had massive claws where fingers should be. The creature slowly turns to hold one of Ben's torn off arms in its grasp. Blood drips from its skeleton-like mouth and on to the snow, causing it to become a light red color. Its piercing red eyes with black pupils staring menacingly.

Mick's gun begins to shake as his mouth drops at the sight of the thing. Without thought, he drops the weapon and his flashlight and takes off at a sprint back around the house through the snow back towards the car. Without the car's headlights now, he can only see what the moon will let him. Jumping into the driver's side seat, he attempts to start the vehicle. Nothing happens.

"Shit. SHIT!"

Quickly getting out of the car, he looks at the engine to see that the hood was punctured and that it is leaking fluids. A horrific screech echoes throughout the woods as he moves back into the car to grab the keys and shuffles towards the trunk. Fumbling the keys in his icy hands, he finds the trunk key and unlocks the trunk. Grabbing the shotgun lying in the trunk, he quickly opens ammo can full of buckshot. Juggling the shot in his hands, he drops a few in snow as he does his best to quickly load the shotgun. One shell slides in, then the second.

"Mick… Mick Gorski."

Mick's hands stop in the middle of loading the shotgun.

"Detective? Detective Barnes?"

"It's me, Mick."

Mick lets go of the shotgun and turns to see a figure standing behind him.

"Barnes, you… you have been missing almost eight years! How…"

"It's me, Mick."

"Barnes… I don't know how… we gotta get out of here! Something got my partner…"

"Mick, it's me."

Mick stops as his name is repeated, he turns and grabs a flashlight out of the truck and turns it on. As he turns to face Barnes, his flashlight reveals the terrifying truth. Another one of those creatures stands before him, salivating through his skeleton mouth. Its teeth reassemble that of a human. Its soulless red eyes focused on him intensely. Its mouth opens as it speaks the human language.

"It's me, Mick."

Mick screams at the top of his lungs. Grabbing the shotgun once again, he fires it at the creature that is advancing upon him quickly without aiming. The shot hits the transformed Detective Barnes in the shoulder as his right side is pushed back from the blast. Mick shoulders the shotgun and aims for another shot before hearing a loud metal crunch behind him. Slowly turning to look behind him, he sees that the creature who devoured Ben is now drooling blood from its mouth on top of the car.

In an instant, Mick is ambushed by both creatures without hesitation. They began to slaughter him alive until his screaming subsides. Devouring their pray, like rabid animals, a lone call sounds to them from deep within the dark woods, stopping their feast of human flesh. Looking upon each other, they make an unearthly hollow noise.

The one that attacked Ben begins to feast again as Barnes turns toward the call. Looking at the creature feasting, it opens its mouth slightly.

"Cyles."

The creature stops eating and looks at Barnes. It quickly grabs Mick's body and takes off at abnormal speeds into the dark forest. Barnes immediately follows in pursuit. The two creatures move quickly throughout the frozen woods. In a matter of minutes, they are back to where it all began—the cave in the woods. A fire still burned in the clearing giving light to everything around them. They stood in front of the cave and waited in silence.

The beast they have come to serve appears out of the cave, speaking to them.

"My children. I have had a vision."

It walks as if it is floating towards them. Cyles drops what is left of micks' body off to the side of him. They both present their heads as it places its hands gently on their skulls. Instantly, Barnes is overcome with visions of a young child that will be born not too far from here. The vision shows that he will be chosen by God and cause great turmoil for the beast and creatures. If not stopped, he could be the end of them and their master.

They both awake once again in the forest clearing in front of the cave, they let out a long screech in anger.

"It's alright, my children," the beast says as it caresses them.

"You have been chosen and will hunt and torment this child and then… eat him."

The two let out excited howls as saliva drips from their mouths on to the sandy shores of the creek bed.

CHAPTER 12

Out of the Dark Woods

Many seasons pass after the death of the two police officers. Even after the search party was called off, some people say that their deaths were at the hands of Cyles Deckler, the one responsible for the riverside road massacre. Eventually, what is true is gone, and now there only stands what is known. Rumors engulf Dolittle Hill forest, and it becomes the story of legend, myth, and then, eventually forgotten. Sheriff Jones, Detective Barnes, becomes long forgotten as well, and the abandoned riverside road home of Cyles and Mae Deckler deteriorates over time as new forest growth engulfs the house and claims it as its own, but our story continues.

Creatures, once known as Barnes and Cyles, move quickly through the woods in silence as they sense the presence of small, vulnerable prey walking alone just outside the wood line at night. They come to a halt as the smell intensifies, and a single light shines from outside the woods. The creatures stick to the shadows avoiding the putrid light as much as possible, but the smell draws them in and enslaves them with hunger. Unearthly hollow noises erupt from what's left of their throats as their excitement intensifies. They see the outline of the pray as it comes to a halt right before entering a path through the woods.

"Montana?" A worried male child's voice asks timidly.

They began to stalk their prey, saliva drooling from their skull mouths at the thought of the flesh before them.

"Montana, get out here!" The boy calls more demandingly this time.

Setting up an ambush, Barnes keeps the boy's focus on him hidden in the woods by creating a growling sound. Cyles circles around, unseen and unheard to attack from behind.

The boy sensing their advancement, bends down quickly and picks up a stick and aims it wildly.

"Get out of here!" He yells, taking one step backward.

"I am warning you, dammit!"

As Cyles creeps up on the boy from behind, blinded by his intense hunger, steps on a stick lying in the grass. The boy turns quickly as Cyles pauses; eyes focused. The boy begins to panic as he knows he is being cornered like prey to a trap.

With little hesitation, the boy begins to scream loudly and takes off at a sprint through the woods. The creatures give chase, hot on the child's tail.

<u>Our story continues in Out of the Dark Woods, thank you for your support and sweet nightmares.</u>

Out of the Dark Woods
Second book of the series

A psychological thriller about a child living in rural southern Indiana experiencing unusual hauntings by the creatures of the woods. Are they real, or just a fabrication of the mind?

For sale on Amazon and Barnes and Noble websites.

ABOUT THE AUTHOR

Branden Smith is a self-published author of the Out of the Dark Woods series. Graduated from Saint Leo University and currently serving in the U.S. Navy, he focuses on the thriller and fantasy genres. If you would like to stay up to date on all his book releases, make sure to join his email list at matthew.b.smithbooks@gmail.com

Website: https://matthewbsmithbooks.wixsite.com/brandensmith
Facebook: @BrandenSmithbooks
Amazon: amazon.com/author/brandensmith

Printed in Great Britain
by Amazon